MW01170705

THE LONEWOLF:

A Paranormal Novel

ANNA G. BERRY

CONTENTS

Copyright © 2021 by Anna G. Berry

All rights reserved. This book or any portion thereof may not be reproduced or used in any manner whatsoever without the express written permission of the publisher except for the use of brief quotations in a book review or scholarly journal.

ISBN

❀ Created with Vellum

To my husband, Andy, who has supported me through everything.

PROLOGUE

CLAUDIA

I NEVER THOUGHT I would be the one to run my dad's pack at such an early age. You see, my mom and dad were murdered when I was sixteen. I remembered that my brother had to call and tell me because I was away at the time of their murder. He found them. I was so crushed when Paul called and told me what had happened. I could not get out of bed for a day and half. Thank God my brother Paul was there to help me get through the pain and anguish of losing our parents.

It took some time for the other packs to take me and Paul seriously since we were only kids, but they eventually warmed up to us and helped us when we needed it.

It had been a mystery to me as to who killed my parents until I got into the Alpha council and went to my first meeting. I had to wait until I turned eighteen to join the Alpha Council. The rules were strict, and you also could not join unless you were a pure-blood wolf and the Alpha of your pack.

The pure bloods are split up in the wolf world. There were the pure bloods of Europe and pure bloods of America. The pure bloods from Europe had hailed from Romania and Ireland for centuries. They were a lot bigger than their American counterparts. The American pure bloods hailed from the South and the Midwest, South Carolina and Iowa. Eye color was especially important in the wolf realm. The purple eyes from an American showed royalty. Most could be found in South Carolina, where I was from. Green eyes signified royalty in the European clan, I had heard of only one family with those color eyes.

My brother and I had purple eyes and we were the only two that I knew of, aside from our dad, that kept our eye color when we shifted. Everyone else's eyes changed to a honey color as they shifted. You see, my family was different. There was something about having purple eyes that allowed us to keep our color. I never knew why, and no one told me.

I had not met anyone from the European royals, that I was aware of. There were two families from what I had heard, one from Ireland and the other one from Romania. I heard that the Irish were more laid back and the Romanians were the dangerous ones. The ones to look out for. It was like how the Midwestern pack in America was pretty laid back and my pack, from the South, was the dangerous one.

Once I heard about the Romanian pack, I wanted to meet them so that I could pick their brains on fighting techniques.

Little did I know at the time that those techniques would come in handy sooner rather than later.

"Claudia who do you think our mate will be? Do you think we will ever find our mate?" my wolf, Noah asked me, as she he broke me out of my thoughts.

I sighed, "Not with the way our life is going, but you never know. I hope that if we do, you will shut up about it." I rolled my eyes to the ceiling.

"I hope he's hot," Noah said.

I rolled my eyes again. Noah is my wolf side. When I shifted into my wolf, she was in control. Also, when I got mad, she came out and handled the situation.

I was the youngest in the pack to shift and become in tune with my wolf. I was six when I first shifted. I remembered my mom and dad were surprised when it happened. Typically, wolves shift when they hit puberty and normally it was at a full moon, but when I first shifted it was during a new moon.

Paul was a bit hurt when it happened because he had not shifted yet, but the next full moon he went through his first shift. Our parents kept us sheltered because they did not want anyone to use us at such an early age.

They were very protective of us when we were younger. When they died, my brother became just as protective as they were. I was never alone. I always had someone with me.

Our parents' friend, Waylon, was around a lot after our parents died as well. I never could understand why, and neither could Paul. It had been nice to have a familiar face around, though. He helped us out a lot through the years, even though I could not figure out why. I didn't dwell on it, though. I was the youngest person to become Alpha in centuries and I needed all the help I could get. I had not realized that I would be getting help from the enemy. I also didn't realize that the one person I put all my trust in would be the one out to get me.

THERE WAS something about cemeteries that had always made things fall right into place for me. It made it the perfect place to meet my Betas, who were my brother, Paul, and Marco. My brother was my second in command while Marco was my third in command. Marco stepped in when Paul was not available. They were both amazing and extremely important to me. They were there for me when no one else was and very loyal. My brother respected me, and he was also my protector. Marco was incredible, but he questioned me sometimes and he challenged me on my decisions with the pack most of the time. I knew how to handle him though, and I knew it was just because he cared about me and the pack.

Before we get into it anymore, let me introduce myself. My name is Claudia Stonewell, and I am the Alpha to the most dangerous pack in the south. I expanded into every southern state in the United States.

You might be wondering why I am the Alpha and not my

brother. When my brother was born, our dad noticed that he didn't carry the Alpha traits, so our mother and father decided to have another child, but when they found out that I was a girl, they didn't know what to do.

When I was about five, they noticed that I was always barking orders at my brother, he was eight at the time. That was when they realized that I was the next Alpha to take over the pack. So, my dad had my brother do research on other packs and their numbers and where their territory was well as their training techniques.

I, on the other hand, went with Dad to meetings so that I could learn what it took to be an Alpha. Other Alphas tried to challenge my dad and I by trying to take over the pack or telling my dad that he was crazy to let a female become Alpha. I always proved that I was next in line to run Cold-stone Pack and expand it. With the help of my brother, we have become extremely dangerous.

My best friend, Lavender, is a werewolf as well. She had been my best friend since we were four years old. She was like a sister to me and I could talk to her about anything. The only part that I really hated was that I often felt like the third wheel when we went out anywhere. Almost everyone in the pack had a mate, aside from me. Then again, I never spent my time looking for one. I knew that when I found him, he would be the man that I had been dreaming about. I was a hopeless romantic. I saw how Paul was with Abby and how Lavender was with Max, and I yearned for that.

As I came to the grave site where my family was buried, I found it to be a bit cold for a fall evening in Charleston. There were leaves on the ground everywhere I looked. The streets were so deserted that it made the graveyard even more spooky. I could hear a dog barking in the distance and a car starting somewhere to the left of me.

I could see my mother's gravestone to the right of my father's, just a few feet from where I stood. I decided to sit down next to my grandfather and father's gravestones and made myself comfortable.

When I looked up, I saw Marco as he made his way towards me.

"Hello, Alpha," Marco said as he approached me.

"Hello Marco, I hope he's on time. I really don't like being kept waiting," I said as I lit a cigarette.

"I know. May I have a cigarette Alpha Stonewell?" he asked, looking everywhere but at me. He only called me by my last name when he was scared about something. I let out a cough. He looked down at me and I made a motion for him to sit down next to me.

"Yes, here you go." I handed him a cigarette after he sat down.

"Have you heard from your brother since he called you last?" Marco asked as he lit the tip of his cigarette and inhaled.

"No, I haven't," I responded.

"He only told me that both of us should meet here and he'd explain what's going on when he got here." I looked around, hoping he was walking our way. No such luck.

Marco never really liked my brother. They fought over Abby before Marco met Marisol. Marco was cordial towards

Paul because he knew if he weren't, he would have to answer to me. Marco was afraid of both my brother and me, and rightfully so. He did well to just follow our orders and not show disrespect.

I heard someone walking towards us. I looked up and elbowed Marco to do the same. As the figure got closer, I could see that it was my brother walking toward us, so I stood up and Marco followed suit.

"Hey there, Alpha sister. Hello, Marco. How's everything been since I've been in Canada?" Paul asked as he wrapped me up in a bear hug.

"I've been good, and everyone is doing well. What did you want to talk about that you couldn't tell me over the phone?" I asked him as I took a drag from my cigarette. I knew that it must have been important, or he would have told me on the phone.

"Well Alpha, Carson wants to meet you and me tomorrow for lunch to talk and go over a few things." He looked at me.

"We have to tell the rest of the pack," Marco said, looking between Paul and me.

"That is fine, we can tell them tonight. Paul, why does he want to meet us now? What time and where does he want to meet?" I asked.

"At twelve in the afternoon tomorrow at the China Sun in the neutral zone. He really didn't say why he wanted to us now though," Paul smiled.

"Okay, let's go back to the pack house and let everyone know," I said, brushing the dirt off my clothes. I walked to the woods and took off running.

2

THE PACK HOUSE wasn't that far from the cemetery, plus I needed the run to clear my head. Carson was the new kid in town. The Rivershore pack was led by a good family friend that passed away right before our parents did, according to Paul. When they passed away it was left to the Alpha's brother, as one kid was at school at the time and the other one was not an Alpha. The uncle recently decided to hand the pack over to his nephew, who I had not met yet, or had I? My memory from when I was little was a bit fuzzy. I heard stories from the girls in other packs that he was the hottest man in his territory. I also heard that Carson's Beta was good looking too.

Word was that neither of them had mates and every girl wanted to fill that position. I also heard that Carson was covered in tattoos and piercings, which were my weakness. I was curious to meet them so I could see what all the fuss was about.

9

Before long, I stood outside of the house, admiring it. There were wide windows along the back. The front had one wall of windows and the door was tucked into a covered patio. The second floor of the house had one big bay window. I loved how big it was and how open all the windows made it feel on the inside. It made it feel like I was still outside, near the woods.

Inside, everyone was listening to loud music and hanging out. I walked over to the stereo and turned it down. Everyone stopped what they were doing and looked at me. Standing straight up I cleared my throat and tried to relax.

"I will be going to meet Alpha Carson of the Rivershore pack to talk about a few things tomorrow. While we are gone, I need y'all to keep training and doing patrols. This is our first meeting with the Rivershore pack since they got a new Alpha, so this is especially important," I said as I looked around the room and made eye contact with each person.

"Yes Alpha," they all said in unison.

"Good! You may go back to do whatever y'all were doing," I said as I waved my hand and walked towards my room.

The living room was open to the kitchen and dining room. To the right of the kitchen was an open staircase. It looked like the stairs were floating on air. I looked straight out into the backyard, through the large windows and admired the green trees and grass. Outside was where I belonged. If I had to be inside, I preferred to be in a house of windows, like my own.

I walked up the stairs to my room. Doors lined the

hallway upstairs with gray walls accenting the wood of the doors. There were eleven bedrooms, a library, and the laundry room to the left at the top of the stairs. I also had an office amongst all the bedrooms on the upper level of the home.

My room had a four-poster bed in the middle of the room as well as a bay window. On the left side of the room was my closet and my bathroom. I shuffled over to my bed and sat down. I couldn't stop thinking about Carson and what everyone said about him.

His name was so familiar. Why though? It wasn't because I had heard his name come up in conversations in the past. It was like his name was echoing in my mind. Like there was some memory that we had that I can't seem to find inside of my mind.

Why does he want to meet? What does he want? More territory? Did one of my wolves enter his territory?

My mind was full of questions and I desperately wanted to sort them out. There was a knock at my door, disrupting my thoughts.

"Who is it?" I asked.

"It's me, Claudia. Can I come in?" I heard my best friend ask from the other side of the door.

"Yes, I need someone to help clear my head," I said. She opened the door and walked in.

"What's going on girl?" she asked as she sat down on my bed next to me.

"It's this meeting tomorrow. We have not met yet, that I know of, and he took over almost three years ago. When we do talk, it has always been on the phone. I am just wondering what he wants or if there is something going on that I do not know about yet. I just don't get why he wants to meet now. Also, his name sounds very familiar, like we met a long time ago or something. If that even makes sense." I knew I was rambling; it was a nervous habit.

"Girl you need to relax and get some sleep. It will be okay. Paul is going to be there, and he is not going to let anything happen to his sister and our Alpha. Let us talk more tomorrow after the meeting, okay?" She hugged me.

"Yeah, that sounds good. I'm going to need a girl day after this," I said looking at my hands.

"Maybe Carson will be your mate," she said suddenly with a devilish grin and a wink.

I let a giggle escape and gave her another hug.

"See, this is why you are my best friend. You know what to do to make me smile, even when I don't feel like it. Do you know something that I don't?"

"I'm glad but I'm serious about you getting some sleep. Maybe I do, but that is for you to find out on your own," she said sternly before giving me a kiss on the cheek and hopping off the bed. She walked to the door and slowly turned towards me just before walking out.

"Goodnight Claudia." She turned off the light and closed the door. I felt a lot better after talking to Lavender. She made me feel good about going to the meeting tomorrow. I was not sure why I had been so nervous in the first place. I was alone in complete darkness and it doesn't take long for me to drift off to sleep.

I was in the clearing at the middle of the property at dusk. I walked out to the middle to see a tall, dark and handsome figure; he took my breath away. There were tattoos all over him and he had his ears pierced along with his nose and lip. He was wearing a tank top and black ripped jeans with a pair of gray chucks. He was smoking a cigarette and he had his jet-black hair parted to one side. He looked up and locked eyes with me, his deep green eyes were beautiful, I wanted to reach out and touch him, but I thought better of it. He had a tattoo that looks just like mine but his was on his wrist while mine was on my neck. I kept trying to get a better view of the stranger, but his face seemed to always be obscured from my view. I couldn't quite make out his face, but those eyes…they seared into my mind so that I would never forget them.

I woke up in the morning with the feeling that someone was staring at me. I opened my eyes slowly to see my brother standing in my bedroom gazing at me.

"What's wrong?" I asked as I sat up.

"It's ten thirty in the morning and we have a meeting at twelve that we can't be late for." He looked down at his phone.

"Okay, I'm getting up, go away so I can change." I waved my hand at him.

He laughed but turned and left the room so I could get ready for the day. I walked into my closet so that I could figure out what to wear, but nothing appealed to me. I did not want to look too cute where they did not take me seriously as an Alpha, but I also didn't want to seem so hardened that I didn't seem feminine. Even though I was an Alpha, I was still a girl and I liked to look good.

I called out for the girls to come help me by mind-linking to all of them, "I need you guys help with an outfit. I can't think of anything."

That was one of the perks of being in a pack. We could mind-link to each other and communicate without ever opening our mouths. After a moment, all six of them shuffled into my room, one by one.

"Sit," Lavender said.

I did as I was told and sat at the vanity inside my closet. They got to work putting an outfit together for me. Abby and Bleu handed me a black crop top, a red flannel shirt, tight red jeans, and black and red Vans. I put it on, and I was impressed. The outfit really made my fair skin shine. My purple eyes were something that stood out for obvious reasons, purple eyes weren't common, but also because my skin was pale, so they really popped.

The top had my big boobs popping out and the flannel showed off my tiny figure. I had curves for days and this outfit was showing each one of them. The red jeans showed my long-muscled legs and made it look as though I had an ass. I loved it.

Lavender had me sit back down at the vanity. "Let's leave it down today, yeah?"

I nodded. "You're the boss."

I winked at her as she ran a brush through my natural red hair. It was the kind of red that a lot of girls dreamed of having and the natural wave and shine to it makes it that much better.

Once I was ready, I gave each of the girls a hug. "Thank you for helping! I don't know what I would do without you."

I walked out into the hall and found Paul by the front door, ready to leave. He looked annoyed as he asked, "Are you ready?"

"Yes, sorry I couldn't find anything to wear," I said.

"It's eleven now, we need to leave, or we'll be late," he said, rolling his eyes.

"Who's the Alpha in this pack?" I asked with a giggle.

He rolled his eyes again and walked out the door. I looked at Abby who had walked up behind me, but she just shrugged her shoulders, and I knew that there weren't any issues between them.

"I'll talk to him," I told her as I walked out the door. She closed it behind me as I made my way to the car.

"Hey what's going on? You seem off and I don't like it," I said as I climbed into the passenger seat.

"It's Marco. He doesn't think we should go and meet Carson. I told him it was not his decision. He's starting to piss me off," he said as he gripped the steering wheel.

"Don't let him get to you right now. Just focus on the meeting. I'll deal with him when we get back," I told my brother 1 as I rubbed his arms like I would do when we were little.

He smiled at me and started the car. We decided to take his car which was a 2018 Audi R8 in matte black. It was an amazing car, but he mainly liked it because it could reach high speeds in the matter of seconds.

We made small talk as he drove, but I was too nervous to comprehend half of it. I started to fidget in my seat as we got closer to the restaurant.

"What's going on with you, my Lilly Pad?" he asked, calling me by my nickname. He had been calling me that since we were little, and I smiled a bit at the sound of it.

"Just nervous about this meeting, that's all," I responded.

"Well, suck it up because we're here already," he laughed as he turned the car off after parking it.

I unbuckled my seat belt and rolled my eyes in his direction. Sometimes, I wanted to strangle him for his smart-ass remarks. I did not want to focus on that now, though. Paul could try to get under my skin all he wanted. I was not planning on letting his brotherly tactics get to me, though.

Instead, I took a deep breath before gathering the courage to walk towards the restaurant.

3 CLAUDIA

WE WALKED into the restaurant which was a little hole in the wall that had amazing food. It was lit well, and there were only four other customers inside. A couple in the left corner in the back and two guys sitting in a booth to the right in a corner.

I was suddenly hit with the smell of aftershave, peppermint, and the woods after a long rain. I took a step back; it was the most amazing smell; it was also remarkably familiar as well. I could feel Paul's eyes on me. The wolf in me caused my head to lift as I inhaled deeply again.

"Are you okay?" he asked, looking at me with a worried expression.

"Yeah, let us get this over with. Where are they sitting at?" I asked, shaking my head, trying to push the mouthwatering smell out of my mind.

He gave me another questioning look but did not comment on it. He ushered me towards the booth in the back right corner of the restaurant. As we got closer, the heavenly scent got stronger and stronger. It was making me dizzy with happiness and I was not sure why.

We were close enough to the booth now, so I could see who was sitting in it. I locked eyes with a man who seemed to have been sculpted by God himself. He stood up and my eyes followed his every move. He was about six foot three, maybe more, and I could tell he worked out a lot. I could see every muscle rippling through his shirt. His hair was jet black laying towards the right and his eyes were a familiar deep green color and that was what held me in place. He was covered in tattoos and he had his ears, nose, and lip pierced. It was eerily familiar, and I needed to keep my head straight.

My jaw dropped. Alpha Carson was better looking than I had imagined after hearing the gossip around town about him. I did not know what to say, but I held out my hand for him to shake.

"That's our mate!" I heard my inner wolf cry.

"We don't know that yet, now shh," I told her in my head.

"Hello, Alpha Claudia and Beta Paul. I'm Alpha Carson and this is my Beta, Harper," Carson said as he waved a hand to the other guy with him.

He took my hand and at his touch it felt as though electricity was shooting through my body. We gazed at each other for a few seconds before letting go.

Paul tapped me on the shoulder and cleared his throat to get my attention. I tore my gaze away from the handsome being in front of me and looked at my brother.

"Want to get in the booth?" he asked, looking at me like I was crazy.

I nodded my head and slid across the leathery fabric of the booth and looked at the menu. I forced myself not to stare at the man who was now sitting across from me as I selected what I was going to eat.

The waitress came by, she was in awe of the guys. She kept making sweet eyes at Carson and his Beta. I managed to place my order without looking across the booth. I ordered a Root Beer and the lunch special. I waited for the guys to place their order and made a point to look every-where but across the table, but when the waitress left, I glanced up to see another God-like man sitting diagonally from me. I was too distracted by Carson to really look at his Beta.

This man was a few inches shorter than Carson. He, like Carson, was covered in tattoos and had the same piercings, too. The only difference was he had lighter black, almost slate gray hair and his eyes were lighter green. I could not stop thinking that they reminded me of a summer meadow, like the one in my dreams and the one out in the woods behind the house. It was more so Carson's eyes than Harper's.

"Let's get this over with, shall we?" Paul was the first to speak.

"You don't let your Alpha talk?" Carson asked while staring intently at me. To me, his voice sounded like heaven. It was thick and gravely, and it was giving me goosebumps.

"He's my brother. I do not mind when he takes control of the conversation from time to time. Why did you want to meet?" I asked, waving my hand a bit annoyed at my wolf, Noah, who would not shut up about Carson.

"Okay, if you want to get down to business, then I want to talk about expanding my territory. I want to make a deal so that we don't harm each other when we cross over," said Carson.

"Okay, we can talk about that. I am open to your suggestions and ideas. Are you seeing anyone?" I asked before I could stop myself.

All three of them looked at me, surprised at the unexpected question. I growled at Noah who I knew had a big grin on her face. It wasn't what I wanted to ask him, but it was out in the open now.

"I'm sorry, what I meant to say was, where did you want to expand to?" I asked, gathering myself.

"No, I am not seeing anyone. I would like to expand to the area we are in right now, actually," Carson said, giving me a wink and letting out a small chuckle.

"I'll have to think about it. Being that it is close to my pack line and me being head Alpha of the state, I will go over the terms. I just want to make sure that it is safe for everyone involved. I will let you know," I said giving the two men a shy smile.

"Let me know about what? The part about me not seeing anyone, or the territory?" Carson asked with a laugh.

"Both." The word came out of my mouth before I could stop myself, once again.

"Awesome," he said giving me a crooked smile.

"Why did you want to meet now after being in control of

the pack for a little over three years? What changed your mind?" I asked a bit harsher than I meant to be.

"You. I wanted to see what all the fuss was about. You have quite the reputation, pisoi." He gave me a smirk.

"What do you mean?" I didn't know how to respond to that statement.

"You have been talked about. How beautiful you are, and that you are quite the badass." He smirked again, leaving a foreign feeling in me.

I blushed under his gaze and became highly aware that Paul and Harper were staring at the two of us. Thank God our food came at that moment. I started to eat before I could say something else that made me want nothing more than to crawl under the table.

I half listened as the guys started to talk about other things. A few minutes later, I finished eating but the guys were still talking. While they were distracted, I decided to have a little talk with my wolf about what had happened.

"What the hell was that about?" I asked her. Being a wolf, I could talk to Noah, my wolf side, any time I wanted.

Sometimes she could take control of my human form, too. Mostly when I was angry but today, she was beginning to be a nuisance more than anything.

"He's our mate!" Noah yelled at me.

"Who is? Carson or Harper?" I asked her.

"The cocky one, duh. Just say his name. Say 'Carson is my mate,'" she said to me.

"He's not cocky. Wait, out loud?" I started to fidget in my seat again.

"Yes, stop being in denial that Carson is our mate!" she said. She was getting inpatient with me.

I continued to fidget in my seat and did not realize I had caught the attention of the guys.

"Carson is my mate. Are you happy?" I asked out loud, rolling my eyes.

"Yes. Oh, he heard you by the way," she sang gleefully.

I looked up to see three set of eyes on me, one of them purple and the other two green. I blushed and looked down at my hands. I put my head on the table and cursed Noah before getting up and walking outside without another word. I needed a cigarette to calm myself, and fast.

The fresh air hit my face once I made it outside and I lit my cigarette. I took a long drag and felt the tension leaving my body as I heard footsteps coming up behind me. The same heavenly smell that I noticed in the restaurant, hit me again. Without looking, I knew who it was.

"Can I bum one?" the voice asked from behind me.

"Sure." I turned around to see Carson gazing at me again.

"Can I...?" he asked, gesturing toward my favorite black lighter with skulls and roses on it. I handed it over to him and watched him light his cigarette.

"Sorry about my little outburst," I said after he handed the lighter back to me. I looked down and took a long drag from my cigarette.

"Would it make it better if I said that Claudia is my mate?" he bent down and whispered in my ear. My cheeks warmed at the feel of his breath against my ear. Again, the same foreign feeling came up.

"My wolf was driving me crazy, so I said it to make her shut up," I said, playing it cool.

"So, you didn't mean it?" he asked as he walked to stand in front of me.

"I did, I mean… Anyway…" I let my sentence drop off. I couldn't understand why I was so flustered around him, but he made me forget how to act normal, that was for sure.

He chuckled, "Plus, you don't want to be here when my wolf comes out. He can be bit full of himself." He gave me a wink.

"I think I can handle myself with your wolf. If he is anything like you," I said.

"We'll have to test that theory one day. So, tell me about yourself, my beautiful mate." He let out another chuckle.

I took another drag and looked around, not really wanting to tell this guy my life story, but something was making me tell him whatever he wanted to hear, and it was not Noah.

"Not much to say, my brother Paul and I are the only ones from my family that are alive. He is my Beta even though he is three years older than me. When my father passed away six years ago, I took over and became Alpha. I grew up here, in South Carolina. I've never had a boyfriend because my dad and brother were always so protective, so, I never found anyone, or had a reason to," I finished. I looked up at him and those green eyes bored into mine.

"So, your brother is your Beta? My brother is mine, also. My uncle gave me the pack about three years ago. I'm from here as well but moved to go to college. About seven years ago when my uncle got sick, I came back down here," he said.

"Have you ever had a girlfriend?" I blurted out.

I could have kicked myself. What was wrong with me? I thought as I wondered why I kept blurting stupid shit out.

He smirked at me before answering. "I've had my fair share of ladies but none that made me want to know more about them, like you do," he said, taking a drag from his cigarette.

"Wait... really? I'm not that interesting," I said as I shrugged my shoulders.

"Yes, really. There is something about you that is remarkably familiar. Is that a surprise?" He tilted his head and blew smoke out of the right corner of his mouth.

I shook my head, unable to said anything. We stood there and finished our smoke break in silence. I turned to let him know that I was heading back into the restaurant, but our eyes locked and I forgot what I was going to said. The next thing I knew, he was inches from my face, and I could smell the aftershave and the smell of the woods after a heavy rain. The nicotine on his breath mixed with the peppermint was intoxicating.

I did not know what had come over me, but I closed the inches and put my lips on his. We lost ourselves in the kiss. I parted my lips and let him explore my mouth, while I did the same with his. His taste was blissful, the peppermint taste was at the tip of my tongue and I could not get enough.

He drew back and gazed down at me. "You taste amazing. I had to stop before I had my way with you right here." He winked at me before giving me a kiss on my temple.

"You taste as good as you smell," I said as I blushed.

"We should go back. I just came out to see if you were okay." He ran his hand through his hair.

"Yeah, we should. Thank you for coming to see if I was okay." I squeezed by him and walked through the door of the restaurant with him trailing behind me.

We made it to the booth, and I saw Paul looking at me with curiosity burning in his eyes.

"Is everything okay?" Harper asked Carson as we sat back down in the booth.

"Yeah, Harper. We will have to wait until Alpha Claudia makes her mind up," Carson said while smiling at me. I blushed for the millionth time and looked down at my hands.

"Okay, that's fine. Let's go back home. Those chicks are waiting on us. They're fine as hell and I want fuck some bitches," Harper said nonchalantly as he nudged Carson out of the booth so he could get up.

"I'm not interested in those girls," Carson said sharply to Harper.

"Okay, your loss. I'll meet you at the car." Harper said as he walked towards the front of the restaurant and then out the door. Paul glanced between Carson and I curiously before following Harper out of the restaurant.

"So, before you go, are we mates?" I asked him.

"Yes Pisoi. There is a strong connection between us. I think we are mates," he said.

"Pisoi?" I asked.

"It means Kitten in Romanian," he explained with a wink. I smiled and then my smile turned to a frown.

"Hey, don't look like that, I'm yours and no one else okay," Carson whispered in my ear.

"I know just... I don't like that my mate will be in a house full of sluts," I said letting out a growl.

"If it makes you feel better, I will text you till we both fall asleep. Your brother has my number," he said.

He bent down and gave me another kiss on my temple. I shook my head as he smiled down on me. He grabbed my hand and we walked out of the restaurant together.

4 CLAUDIA

PAUL WAS LEANING against the car and I could see Harper leaning against a red matte Lamborghini, smoking a cigarette a few feet away. I turned my eyes back to Paul and see that he's glaring at Carson.

I dropped Carson's hand and got in the car without looking back at him. Paul climbed into the driver's seat and drove off. I could feel Paul's eyes on me, but I ignored him.

"So, Carson, huh?" he asked.

"Yes," I replied.

"What took you guys so long on your smoke break earlier?" he asked, taking his eyes off the road to look at me.

"We kissed, and it was amazing. I wanted to start ripping his clothes off right then and there," I started to ramble. I blushed when I realized I might have shared too much with my brother.

"Well, he definitely is your mate; I was like that when I met Abby. I know that look anywhere," he laughed.

"I don't know what to do. Should I hold off on their expansion so that I can get to know Carson a bit more and see where this goes? Do I give him the expansion because I think he's my mate? But what if this attraction I feel for him is blinding me into making hasty decisions?" I asked Paul.

In this moment, I am a little sister who desperately needed her big brother.

"Why don't you sleep on it and we'll talk about it tomorrow? You promised the girls that you would have a girl's night with them, remember? Try and have fun tonight and take up your Alpha duties again in the morning," he said as he pulled into our driveway.

"Okay, let's meet first thing tomorrow in my office." I put my head in my hands and took a deep breath.

"Everything will be okay my Lilly Pad." Paul gave me a warm smile and kissed me on the forehead.

I gave him a small smile before stepping out of the car. I walked to the front door and turned the doorknob. I stepped inside the house and the first thing I saw was Max, Lavender's mate.

Max was so sexy and if he wasn't the mate of my best friend, I would have believed he was my mate because of my attraction to him. I secretly always had a crush on him, but I would never act on it because of my friendship with Lavender.

I also had a huge crush on Paul's best friend, Ashton. Although, since I met Carson, that crush seemed dimmer, not as full-fledged as it had been a few hours ago. Ashton is a kind soul and hot. He was covered in tattoos, which you already know is my weakness. He belonged to the Break Falls pack in the Midwest.

"Hello? Earth to Claudia." Max waved his hand in my face.

"What? Oh, sorry," I said shaking my head.

"How did everything go?" he asked me.

"I'll tell you all tomorrow. For now, I have a girl's night planned," I said as I gave him a smile. He nodded his head and wandered off.

I walked into the living room to find the girls sitting around, chatting. I suddenly wanted to let everything out all at once, but I looked around the room to see the boys by the pool table playing a game and I knew they would overhear me.

"Are you ready for a girl's night?" I looked at them.

"Yes!! Let's go!!" Lavender said, getting up from the couch.

I let out a laugh at her enthusiasm and made my way to my room with them following behind me. My girls never let me down and I was so thankful for them. When I needed to vent, I could always turn to them.

We piled into my bedroom and everyone made themselves comfortable. I sat in the middle of my bed and Lavender and Abby sat on the sofa that was in the corner of my room. Mikayla, Bleu, and June sat on the other side of the bed. Marisol made herself comfortable on the chair next to the bed and Lorren took a seat next to me on the bed.

I looked down at my hands, highly aware that they were

all looking at me and waited to hear how the meeting went but I didn't know where to begin.

"I found my mate," I blurted out.

They all started talking at once.

"How?" Lavender asked.

"Who is it?" Abby chimed in.

"Tell us everything!" Mikayla squealed.

I couldn't think straight, but despite their dizzying questions, I smiled.

"Let her speak, guys," Marisol said.

"It's Alpha Carson Blackman and that's not all, we made out in the restaurant parking lot," I said in a rush.

I looked around the room to see everyone looking like they were staring at a ghost.

"Wait, Carson is your mate?" Mikayla asked first.

"Yes," I replied.

"The hottest guy on the North side is your mate?" June asked.

"I guess so. Why is that such a shock?" I asked defensively.

"Um, maybe because he's just as dangerous as you," Bleu said simply.

I looked around, everyone seemed to agree with her.

"What's his kill rate and dominance over a pack?" I asked them.

An Alpha's kill rate was the number of kills they had, and their dominance was the number of packs they were in dominance over. The higher the numbers, the more dangerous the Alpha.

"It's not far below yours, he had about six hundred and ten in kills and two hundred in dominance. You have seven hundred in kills and three hundred and twenty in dominance," June said.

"Guys, that's not all. He asked if he could have the neutral zone and a promise that no one from each pack will be harmed if they go to the other's territory," I said, looking around at them. Everyone had a mixture of shock and happiness on their faces.

"We all saw that coming," Abby said and everyone else nodded. I can't help but giggle and they all looked at me like I was on drugs. Before I could have said anything else, my phone chimed, and I saw an unknown number on the screen. I opened the message up.

Unknown: Hello beautiful, this is Carson. After some persuading, your brother gave me your number. Meet me in the woods. Xoxo.

Me: I'll meet you in half an hour.

I smiled and looked up. The girls were still staring at me, so I read them the text. They were all making googly eyes at me as I stood up and looked down at my clothes.

"First, what do you mean that you saw that coming? Also, what should I wear?" I asked, sure that I shouldn't wear the same clothes as earlier.

"What about that pink and black outfit?" asked Bleu.

"Um, his father wrote that if he took over that you would grant him more territory and that no harm would come of it," Lavender said, a bit unsure on how I would take the news.

"Oh, why wasn't I aware of this?" I ran into my closet and grabbed my pink and black jogging outfit and put it on and then I slipped on my running shoes. I came out with my hair in a messy ponytail.

"Damn girl, you fine as hell," Bleu said.

"I don't think Paul saw a reason to tell you. I think he thought that you and Carson would talk about it eventually," Lavender said.

"Oh." I let out a giggle as I opened the bedroom door. The girls followed me, and I was happy that they were okay that I was ditching them on our girl's night, but I think they understood how big of a deal this was for me.

We made our way downstairs and out onto the deck that lead to the back yard. I turned around to said goodbye to them and noticed that Max joined the group.

"Where are you going, Alpha?" he asked, wrapping his arm around Lavender's shoulder.

"Oh, out for a quick nighttime run. It helps me sleep and clear my thoughts. After the day I just had, I need it," I said, letting out a sigh.

"Oh, would you like some company?" he asked, running his hands through his hair.

"Thank you, but I want to be alone this time." I gave him a small smile.

"Okay, just be careful. I'll let Paul know that you went for a run. How long are you going to be? Just in case he asks."

"I'll be back before the sun comes up." I jumped off the

edge of the deck and turned around to wave at them before taking off into the woods.

The clearing was deep in the woods, so I ran at full speed and before long, I made it to the clearing. I could smell him before I could see him. I looked up to find Carson standing in the middle of the clearing and before I could stop myself, I was grinning at him. It was like in my dreams.

5 CLAUDIA

ALL I COULD DO WAS STAND THERE and stare at Carson. In the back of my mind, I was wondering why he wanted to meet me here, but taking him in before me, I couldn't form the question out loud.

"What's the matter, crin mic?" he asked as he tilted his head to the side.

"Nothing. Wait, what did you just call me?" I asked as my head jerked back.

"Crin mic, it means little lily. You look like you're confused about something," he smirked.

I walked further into the meadow and he cocked his head the other way, as if studying me. I could tell that he was watching my every move. I knew I should've been intimidated, but I was not. I was actually enthralled by him.

"What is it that you wanted to talk about that couldn't be said on the phone?" I asked as I came to a stop in front of him.

"I wanted to see you again and I also wanted to talk to

you without anyone else around." He shrugged his shoulders.

I stared at him for a moment in wonder. "This feels so familiar."

He smiled. "I feel the same way. I always had this dream where I see a girl but couldn't see anything else," he said, lighting up a cigarette.

I continued to stare at him. How can this be possible? There must be something that connected us. Could it be my tattoo? I had a tattoo on my neck, and I'd had it for as long as I could remember. It looked like a triangle that was left unfinished with dots on top and below. It also had what looked like a G or a six on the end of the lines that formed the triangle.

"I feel a connection between us, do you feel it, too?" I asked him as I looked at him in his emerald eyes.

"Yeah, I've never felt anything like it, but it feels good, though." He blew smoke up into the air.

I was so memorized by those emerald green eyes that I couldn't respond. I loved the way they shimmered in the moonlight. They looked like jewels sparkling under a beam of light. I'd never seen anything like it before.

"Are you okay?" he asked.

"Yes, sorry. I just don't know what to say." I rubbed my arms to subside the chills that trailed up and down them.

"Are you cold?" He took off his jacket and stepped towards me. He wrapped it around me, and the warmth immediately engulfed me.

"Thanks," I smiled at him. "Tell me about this dream that

you have. I've been having a similar dream also." I pulled the jacket tighter around me and eagerly waited for his response.

He took a long drag from his cigarette before he answered me, "It always starts with me being in the woods and a girl that I can't see. We end up at the lake watching the sunrise, but I can never see her face. I wake up every time I try to get a closer look at her."

I stood there, shocked that he and I had been having the same dream. I could not believe it. I closed my eyes and took a deep breath, exhaling through my mouth.

"I've always had a dream of a guy standing here in the woods, smoking a cigarette, covered in tattoos and piercings. I feel like I am having a strong case of déjà vu right now, like my dream is coming true." I gazed at him.

"I feel the same way. It's crazy that you're the girl in my dreams," he scratched his jaw. I wondered what the dreams meant or why we shared them. Then, I remembered that Lavender was a Voodoo priestess.

Lavender started practicing Voodoo when she was about nine years old. She learned from her grandmother who had thought it would do her some good. She'd has always been very private about it, but I think Voodoo might help Carson and I to better understand what was going on. She was always helping me solve issues I had, and I thought that she could help us figure out what our dreams meant.

"My best friend, Lavender, may be able to help us," I said.

"How would she be able to help?" he asked.

"She has the power to look into dreams. It's a bit weird but also extremely helpful." I shrugged my shoulders and glanced up at him. I laughed at the shocked look on his face.

Voodoo priestesses were not common, especially werewolf Voodoo priestesses. When we needed to, we used that to our advantage when dealing with other packs. I lit a cigarette and focused back on Carson who was still looking at me.

He wasn't wearing a shirt and I was surprised that I'd just now noticed that. The strong sense of déjà vu must have distracted me from his beautiful, naked top half. His chest was covered in tattoos and his nipples were pierced. His muscles were bulging, and he had that defined v-line leading down to his lower half that damn near made me drool. He was the most beautiful thing that I had ever laid eyes on.

"Do you always walk around without a shirt on?" I asked, taking a puff from my cigarette.

"Only at night when I run," he laughed.

"Ah okay, and do you always run in my territory?" I cocked my head to the side.

"Actually, it's the first time that I am awake that I've been here. When I'm here I'm always dreaming, and when I wake up, I automatically go back home," he explained.

"Oh, that's weird." I looked up to see the moon shining bright and the sky filled with sparkling stars. Tonight, there was a full moon. I felt my tattoo begin to burn and pulse. I rubbed the back of my neck where the tattoo was and was surprised to find that it had welted up. I was confused because that had never happened before.

"Are you sure you're okay?" he asked as he watched me rubbing my neck.

"My birth tattoo is burning, and it feels raised. I never had this happened before," I said. Birth tattoos were something that every wolf got at birth and it represented what pack each wolf belonged to.

"May I look at it?" He took a step closer to me.

"Sure." I moved my hair away from my neck.

He ran his fingers along my tattoo and his touch sent chills down my spine. I closed my eyes and an image of a tattoo like mine flashed in my mind. This one had four dots: one on the top, one on the bottom and one on each side. I opened my eyes to find Carson looking at me.

"Do you have a birth tattoo?" I asked.

"Yes, it's on my ankle. I have a tattoo on my wrist, it looks half finished. I must have had it since birth, just like my birth tattoo because I have always had it. It looks like a triangle that was left unfinished with dots on top and below. It also had what looked like a G or a six on the end of the lines that formed the triangle." He bent down and pulled his sock down. It's the same tattoo that I just saw in my mind which was also the same tattoo that I kept seeing in my dreams.

I felt like I had powers that kept trying to surface but couldn't because I didn't know what to do with them.

"Can I ask you something that might be personal?" I asked, looking at his tattoo.

"Sure, go right ahead," he shrugged.

"Do you feel a draw between us?"

"I already told you I did," he grinned at me.

I nodded my head and blushed before continuing, "It's just that, ever since I've been having these dreams, my mood seems to have change as well. My temper is short, I zone out a lot…it's weird. Now that we are here, I have this sense that I am living out my dream. Like you are the man in my dreams, and I can't help but think that it is somehow all connected. The mood swings, zoning out, my temper…" I trailed off and looked at him curiously.

"Now that you mention it, I've been zoning out a lot, too. My temper had been pretty bad as well," he said, scratching his chin again. I was learning that this was a habit for him when he was deep in thought.

"Can you come over tomorrow? We can ask Lavender what this all means?" I asked.

"Sure, I'll come over. I'm curious to see if she knows what is going on between us," he said.

"Want to go to the lake?" I asked making my way to the west side of the meadow.

"Sure, I'll come with you if you like," Carson said as he watched me.

"Sure, just make sure you can keep up," I said back with a giggle.

I took off running and allowed Noah to come out; she was the biggest in the pack, she had snow white fur with black around her dark amethyst eyes. She had brown paws; she was nothing to play with. I looked to my right and saw a jet-black wolf with white on his paws, his eyes a light green jade color. They were beautiful. I couldn't believe how big his wolf was.

Noah is a big wolf at seven and a half feet tall, but he was a tad bit bigger. He must have been eight or eight and a half feet tall. I couldn't really tell with all this running, but I knew he's fucking big.

We both came to a stop at the edge of the shoreline. The view was breathtaking. The sand so white that every time the sun or the moonlight hit it, it sparkled. The water so blue that it was crystal clear during the day and at night it looked black and ominous. The sunsets here were breathtaking. The colors of the sky were blues, blacks, pinks, and orange. The sunrises were amazing as well.

As we came to a stop, I could now see how massive Carson's wolf was. He stood tall at eight and a half feet and his paws were the size of dinner plates. If he really wanted to, he could give me a run for my money in a fight. I looked into those beautiful green eyes of his and saw nothing but kindness and love in them. Noah gave him a small lick and splashed him with her paw.

He turned and splashed her, getting her soaking wet. All I could do was huff at her. She shook it off and tried again, this time giving him all that she had. She got him wet and took off into the water. Carson let out a small growl of annoyance and took off into the water after me. We both swam and splashed each other for a good hour until we decided to get out and head back. I gave him a small lick and took off towards the pack house, happier than I had been in a long time.

6 CARSON

WHAT HAD this female done to me to make me feel this way? I typically didn't give a shit about women, but it was different with her. I wanted so badly to fuck her. I wanted to feel her insides and explore her body, but a part of me wanted to wait so I could give her time to get to know me, and the other part wanted to mark her as mine and keep her safe.

She was the only person that had succeeded to get my head all fucked up like this. Typically, I knew what I wanted, and I stick to it, but she had turned my life upside down. Her smell alone had me all kinds of fucked up. She smelled like raspberries, saltwater, and roses. I could smell her when she walked into the us restaurant earlier today.

She was fine as hell too, so that was a plus, but she'd been different from what I had heard about her. Everyone said she's this big, bad, dangerous wolf who put her pack on the map. All I saw was a sexy woman that was shy and blurted out the first thing that came to mind.

I stared out into the ocean, thinking of how much this girl had my head all over the place. I heard my phone ring which snapped me out of my thoughts.

"Carson speaking, who is this?" I said into the phone.

"Hey boss, it's Harper. I'm just checking to see where you went?" he replied.

I looked around to see the sun was just coming up over the ocean, "I'll be home in three minutes," I said.

"Okay see you then," Harper said before he hung up.

I stuffed my phone back into my pocket and turned around so I could head to the road where my red Lamborghini was parked. The whole mess with this pack from the north was making things hard for me, and now that I may have found my mate in Claudia, it was going to make things a lot more complicated.

I climbed into the car and drove off to the pack house. Everyone should be waking up about now, so I'd tell them we would be having lunch over at Claudia's and that we needed to tell her about the mess with the Light Side pack. It would be interesting to see how she and her pack reacted.

I drove up to the house and turned into the driveway to see Harper, Nikko, and Ryden standing there, waiting for me. None of us had mates and we didn't really care to find one, but then again, Claudia seemed to be just that for me and I didn't it mind one bit.

I got out of the car. "Is everyone up? I need everyone up and in the family room, now. I have some news," I said to them.

"Okay, we can get everyone up. Come on Nikko," Ryden said to me and then looked over at Nikko.

They both walked into the house, pushing each other along the way. We were always rough housing, what could I say? Boys will be boys.

"So, where did you go last night?" Harper asked as we made our way to the front door.

"I went for a run and took a dip in the ocean. You know it helps me think clearly," I said opening the door.

As we walked in, I could see that Nikko and Ryden had already woken everyone up for the meeting. I let out a small sigh as I saw the one person I was hoping to avoid, Yasmeen. She was the only one in the pack that I fucked. That's all we ever did, and it could be a bit much. The sex wasn't that good, but she was always willing. I could tell when I walked in that she had one thing on her mind, and that one thing was me without clothes on, fucking the shit out of her. I, on the other hand, wanted to be fucking the shit out of Claudia and I wanted to put my mark on her, not Yasmeen.

I let out a small cough loud enough for everyone to hear, "Okay everyone I need y'all to shut the fuck up right now. We will be heading to Coldstone pack house in a bit to meet everyone and sign the treaty that will allow everyone to cross the border without getting killed. We also will be discussing the expansion of the territory more. I need everyone to be on their best behavior. I will also tell their Alpha about the conflict we are having with the Light Side pack."

I looked around the room and saw a few of them where a bit shocked and others had sour looks on their faces.

"Yes Alpha!" they all said.

I walked out of the living room and into my room, I needed some time to think alone and I needed a shower. I was only in my room a few minutes before I heard a knock at the door. I didn't even answer it; I didn't want to deal with anyone right now.

I took my shirt off over my head and slipped out of my Vans. I unbuttoned my jeans and kicked them off and then walked into the bathroom when I heard another knock, but I still ignored it.

I started the shower with piping hot water and slipped off my boxers and stepped in. I let the water hit every place on my body as I stood under the water for about twenty minutes before I washed my hair and body. I turned off the water and ran a towel through my hair and wrapped it around my body.

I walked out of the bathroom and into my room to find none other than Yasmeen herself. I walked to my dresser and grabbed a pair of boxers and sweatpants, completely ignoring her. When I dressed, I walked over to my bed and laid down to take a nap before we all had to make the trip to see Claudia and her pack. I did my best to ignore Yasmeen, but she didn't make that easy.

"Hey sexy. Are you ready for some fun?" Yasmeen said as she walked over and grabbed my penis.

"Not in the mood. Go away, I need some sleep before we head over to Coldstone," I said annoyed while I removed her hand.

"Oh, come on. I can do all the work if you want, baby," she purred as she tried to kiss me.

"I said no! Don't call me baby, you're not my mate!" I said as I shoved her off.

"Harper come get Yasmeen before I have to kill her!" I yelled for my brother.

"What has gotten into you? I thought we were on the way to becoming mates?" she asked, getting up from the bed.

"You will never be my mate, get over that. Now go do your training or something!" I told her as I got up and opened the door.

She walked out just as Harper grabbed her arm and dragged her away from me. I slammed the door and locked it. I walked back to my bed and laid back down. I was so tried. Yesterday was a lot for me. I had to control myself so much when I was around Claudia. It took a lot out of me. All I wanted to do when I was around her was put my mark on her and fuck her until she couldn't walk anymore.

I'd never wanted to fuck someone as bad as I wanted to with her. I could feel my birth tattoo start to burn and pulsate, so I sat up to look at it and I saw the dots beginning to go in and out as if they were fading. That was the first time anything like this had happened. I was too tired to think about it right then, though. I needed some sleep before lunch with Claudia, so I decided to worry about it when I woke up. I drifted off to sleep and the next thing I knew I'm standing on the shoreline with Claudia standing next me.

Her beautiful red hair was pulled up in a bun exposing her

neck. I saw the same tattoo that I saw earlier, it's the same as mine but without the dots. She doesn't say anything, nor does she look at me. I reached for her hand but couldn't grasp it.

"Pisoi, what are you doing out here?" I asked her.

"It's beautiful out here, plus this is my land." she replied.

"What's going with you?" I asked a bit confused.

"Nothing is going on," she said pausing a moment before she continued, "Do you know that we are meant to be?"

"Yeah, you are my mate." I was getting more and more confused by the minute.

"We are so much more than just mates; we will be the best," she said as she continued to look out towards the ocean.

"What the hell are you talking about? How the fuck are we more than just mates?" I asked, turning towards her in frustration. She wasn't making sense and I hated that she was talking in riddles.

"The more you ask, the more you will be confused, my love. All will be answered today in the meeting, my sweet wolf," she said as she turned to me.

Before anything else could be said, I awoke. As fast as the dream started, it ended by Harper shaking me awake.

"Dude wake up. We're going to be late," he said as he stepped back.

"Fuck! That was the most confusing dream ever," I said, rubbing my face.

Harper looked at me strangely, but he didn't respond to what I said.

"Get dressed. I'll have everyone get in the proper vehicles, do you want me to drive or are you going to?" he asked as he stopped at the door.

"Thanks. I'll drive. It's not that far from here," I said getting up and walked to my dresser.

"Okay, see you outside," he said as he walked out the door.

I open my shirt drawer and grabbed a random shirt out of it and pulled it over my head. I really wanted to walk in there without a shirt, so I could see the look on Claudia's face. God, I couldn't get her out of my head, she was even in my dreams.

I finished getting ready and then walked outside to see everyone in their vehicles and ready to go. I walked over to Harper and peeked into the car to see if there was anyone else riding with us. I saw Nikko and Ryden in the back seat. I opened the car door and got inside to start the car.

"So, both of you want to ride with us?" I ask, letting out a low laugh.

"They didn't take no for an answer," Harper said as he slid in.

"We want to know what went down with Yasmeen. I never saw her so pissed in my life," Nikko said.

"Nothing. She wanted sex and I wasn't in the mood, but she didn't want to listen," I said as I pulled out of the driveway.

"Damn, what's up with you, dude? You not wanting to fuck Yasmeen who is the easiest lay in town? That isn't like you at all," Ryden said, shaking his head.

"Coldstone is the only pack that had a female as their

Alpha and you just met with her yesterday which is when you started acting weird. Either that chick is your mate, or you are gay and didn't know it," Nikko laughed, piecing things together.

"I'm not gay, I fuck too many girls to be gay," I barked out.

"So, wait the Alpha is your mate?" Nikko asked incredulously.

"I hear she's fine as hell, too, also that she's badass. Got said I'd hit that," Nikko said.

"She's mine! My Mate! Do you hear me?" my wolf, Zeus, growled in my head.

I gripped the steering wheel and increased the speed. I was trying to calm Zeus down; he could kill everyone in the car if I didn't calm us both down.

"Yes Alpha!" they all respond through mind-link.

"Zeus, you need to calm down. Claudia and her pack do not need to meet you just yet. We need Carson back so we can get this meeting over with," Harper said out loud, placing a hand on my shoulder.

"They do not touch Claudia or Noah. They are our mate. I kill anyone who hurts them," Zeus growled out loud in the best English he could.

"Da frate. Te iubesc." Harper responded to Zeus in Romanian, which meant 'yes brother, I love you'.

"Si eu te iubesc." Zeus said as he relaxed.

Zeus calmed down and let me back to the surface as I pulled into Claudia's driveway and put the car in park. I was thankful that Zeus didn't get too out of hand and cause a car wreck. I looked up to see people standing outside, eying the cars as they pulled into the driveway. But all I see is Claudia.

Her beautiful red hair is pulled into two braids that fell over her shoulders. Her stunning dark purple eyes had a shining light in them like they did in the restaurant. I got out and stood beside the car and the rest of my pack following suit. When the boys got out of their cars, they all stood still. I looked over at Claudia and her pack and noticed that three girls to the right of her were mimicking her stance. I let out a small laugh. Claudia really was the head chick in charge around there. So much so that her friends wanted to be just like her.

One of the girls was around the same height as Claudia, with dark brown hair falling down her back and with blue eyes. The second girl was a bit taller with light green eyes and light pink hair that was probably actually brown, judging by her eyebrows. Her hair was in a braid and it fell on her left shoulder. The third girl was also about the same height as Claudia and she had light brown hair that was piled on top of her head with dark blue eyes.

"Alpha Claudia, this is my pack. My male Betas Harper, Nikko, and Ryden. My female Betas Yasmeen, Brooklyn, and Ella. The other members are Jarrod, Kegan, Tabitha, and Willow," I said pointing to everyone.

"Hi, Alpha Carson. It's good to see you again." She had a sparkle in her eye when she talked to me and I loved that shit. "This is my pack. My male Betas Paul, Marco, Maxi, and Emmett. My female Betas Abby, Lavender, Marisol and Bleu.

And this is Mikayla, June, and Lorren," she said pointing at each person.

The three girls that were standing by themselves looked at each other and then at Harper, Nikko and Ryden. I looked over to the guys and they were eying the girls as well. Claudia led her pack into the house, and I gave the guys a look to move into the house with everyone else.

I walked into the house to find myself in a wide-open home. The back of the house was covered in windows and glass doors. The kitchen was set to my left and there were no walls, so it was open and inviting. The cabinets were a cream color, and the countertops were gray, with stainless steel appliances. To my right was an open black steel staircase, behind that was what looked like a laundry room. To the front of me was a family room with two gray sofas and a cherry oak table and a huge flat screen TV.

Everyone moved to the back of the house and through one of the doors where we all walked out and gathered around the back yard where there were tables and chairs set up. We all found seats and got comfortable with Claudia and her pack on the left and my pack and me on the right.

"As everyone knows we are here to discuss business and then we can have lunch and get to know each other more," Claudia said, looking around at everyone.

For the next hour or so, we talked about the treaty and expansion as well as the benefits for everyone. It was a peaceful conversation and by the end, we all seemed to agree.

"There is something that I want to bring you all in on since we are all on the same page. We have an issue with the

Light Side pack. They want our territory and will do everything to take it. We already had to kill three of their members and will have to kill more if we don't get help," I said bluntly.

"That does sound like a problem. I will send a few guys over there to see what's going on. I will also call a meeting with their Alpha, James, to see if I can come to an agreement with him," Claudia said looking at me.

"Thank you. We all appreciate that," I said giving her a nod.

"You're welcome. Can I speak with you in private?" she asked.

"Yeah," I said getting up from the table.

Everyone else scattered, making different groups and chatting with one and another. I walked over to Claudia. She was standing by a Willow Oak tree. I smiled as I got close to her. She was wearing a blue crop top with a gray pencil skirt with white heels. She was driving me crazy with that outfit and I didn't think she knew it.

"What is it that you want to talk about, pisoi?" I asked her.

"It's about our tattoos. Earlier today, my tattoo started to burn and pulse and then four dots in the same place as yours started to appear and disappear. Then I had a dream where I was at the beach with you, but I was speaking weird and I couldn't understand it. I asked Lavender to look into everything if that's okay," she said in one breath.

"I had the same thing happen to me right before my pack and I came here. I would like to know what all this means, too, so I would be interested in what your friend has to say," I said running my left hand through my hair. She nodded and gave me a small smile; she looked past me and waved her hand towards us. I turned around and saw a pretty, light-skinned girl. Her skin was like honey and her hair was all pulled into a ponytail with a headband that held back the stray hairs. She was in a red top with a leather jacket and jeans. She walked up and put out her hand which I took and gave it a shake.

CARSON

I DIDN'T KNOW what to expect but if I could get answers on what the hell is going on, then I was willing to take my chances with Claudia's friend. She led us to a shed of some sort and opened the door. She stood back letting Claudia and me in first.

"Wow this is nice," I said as I looked around.

"Thank you. Claudia was nice enough to make me a place where I can practice," Lavender said with a smile.

I looked at Claudia and she gave me a small smile and grabbed my hand. I returned her smile with one of my own and squeezed her hand. I looked back at Lavender and saw that she was lighting some candles and incense. I won't lie, I was a bit uncomfortable because I was not really into all that Voodoo shit.

"I need both of you to lay down and close your eyes. I need you to relax and try to go to sleep," Lavender said motioning to an area that was filled with blankets and pillows.

We both walked over to the blanket and pillow filled area and laid down. I got in a comfortable position and closed my eyes. Only a few moments later, I got sent to a whole different world. It looked like the waters by Claudia's house, but different. Where the trees normally were there was a stone wall in their place. The water looked dirty and the sand looked brown.

I looked to my right and saw that Claudia had the same confused expression on her face. I looked to my left to see Lavender grinning and then she walked over to the ocean. I felt a pull. like I needed to follow her, so I did. I noticed that Claudia did as well.

"Get into the water," Lavender said in my head. It wasn't mind-link because we weren't in the same pack. This was something different.

I did as I was told and got in.

"Take off your clothes." She spoke in my mind again.

I took everything off and gave my clothes to Lavender. Claudia did the same thing, so I assumed that Lavender was speaking in Claudia's mind too.

I had no idea why she needed our clothes off, but I followed her commands to see if she could figure out this weird connection Claudia and I had. She told us to go deeper into the water, which we did. Suddenly, my ankle started to burn and pulse just like it did earlier. My right wrist started to burn and pulse, too. I looked down to see Claudia's birth tattoo on my wrist going in and out. I felt the need to close my eyes, so I did. I instantly opened them again and I found myself in a house that was run down and looked to be abandoned.

I looked down and noticed that I was still naked. So was Claudia, which I didn't mind one bit. We were standing on a dirty floor and I couldn't see anything beyond the room we were standing in. The room was falling apart. The walls had holes in them, and the ceiling was starting to crumble and cave in.

"I need you both to hold hands and think about your childhood," Lavender said, still annoyingly inside my head.

We grabbed hands and closed our eyes; I started to think about my mom and how she would play with me and my brother. I thought about the time she made up a game that we had to pick out the star that sparkled the brightest. Once we found it, we would have to name it. I smiled at the thought and then started to think about my dad and how he would give my brother and I things to do. He told us once that if we wanted to have his bracelet, we had to spar for it and the winner would get it. The bracelet was special because it was the family crest.

"Now take those memories and let them fuel you to your next task. I need you to think about how those memories made you who you are today," Lavender said next.

I started to think about how both of those memories made my brother and I closer and how we now have similar fighting styles. I also thought about how my dad taught me how to fight for what I wanted and how my mom taught me that it was okay to have big dreams.

"Now I need you to open your eyes and stand back-to-back," she said in a soothing voice.

We closed our eyes and stood back-to-back; neither of us had any idea what was going to happen next. I opened my eyes, and we were standing in the woods. There was so much fog that I couldn't see past my hand. I could feel Claudia next to me, looking around to see where we were.

"Good, now I need you to think about each other," Lavender said.

I thought about how beautiful Claudia was and how short and cute she was and how she didn't let that get in the way of being an Alpha. I thought about how her long, wavy flaming red hair fell around her beautiful heart shaped face and how her dark purple eyes sparkled in the sun but lit up even more in the moonlight. I loved her light skin, making her hair look even brighter and how her mouth curved up when she saw her brother and her eyes change a lighter color, too. I thought about how she smelled and how she tasted. The smell of raspberries, salt-water and roses filled my senses again and I swore it got better each time. She tasted better than she smelled. It was like tasting rose water with a hint of sea salt and rasp-berry jam.

"Now I need you to open your eyes and look at each other," Lavender instructed us.

We opened our eyes and slowly turned around. I got to see those amazingly beautiful eyes of hers and I melted. I wanted to kiss those lips so fucking bad. I wanted to kiss that beautiful neck of hers and I especially wanted to kiss every inch of her body. I couldn't help but feel like I should've been bowing my head at her instead of her bowing down to me.

"Now I want you to kiss each other and I mean really kiss each other. Body to body, lips to lips," Lavender said.

She didn't have to tell me twice. I took my hand and brought it to the back of Claudia's head. We each took a step closer and kissed. I let out a small moan as our lips parted, letting each other in. I could hear Claudia let out a moan as we deepened our kiss. I could feel her beautiful tits on my stomach, and I decided to pick her up. She wrapped her beautiful athletic legs around my waist. When she did that, her kisses got more intense and heated.

I loved this side of her. I matched her intensity as I took my lips to that little neck of hers that I had been dying to taste. I planted a few kisses on it and she went crazy. I came back to her lips as she wrapped her arms around my neck and gently nibbled my bottom lip.

I let out a moan and pulled her off me. "You definitely want me to fuck you, don't you?" I asked.

"I--I'm sorry. I lost it," she said, surprised by her reaction to me.

"I loved it. No need to be sorry," I smirked at her.

"That was excellent, now I need you to come back to me. Close your eyes and think of the shed that you entered in. Good, now open your eyes." Lavender snapped her fingers.

We opened our eyes, and I could see that I still had my clothes on and that we were in Lavender's shed. I turned to see Claudia looking very shyly at me.

"Thank you, Lavender," I told Claudia's friend.

"Anytime. I will be getting what I've found from this visit, tonight. You'll hear back from me in the morning," she told me with a smile. I gave her a smile back and nodded my head.

"Claudia can I have a minute alone with you?" I tapped her on the shoulder.

"Um sure, let's go outside," she said rubbing her left arm.

We walked outside to a small, shaded spot a short distance from the shed. I looked around to see Harper, Ryden and Nikko talking to the three girls from Claudia's pack. I shook my head when I saw Harper lifting his shirt up and making a beautiful brown hair girl laugh.

"What did you want to talk about?" Claudia asked, bringing me back to her.

"Oh, yeah. I would like to take you out to my club on Tuesday night," I said, running my hands through my hair.

"That's cool. I'd love to. Was that all? I would like to get back—" she said but I cut her off by kissing her.

I couldn't take it anymore. I needed to feel her lips on mine. I wanted to mark her right there and then. I could feel Zeus ready to come out, but I held him back.

"Do you want to go for a run?" she asked after we broke apart.

"Yes, I think my wolf would appreciate that," I said.

"What's his name, anyways? Mine is Noah and she's my wild side," she said giggling.

"Mine is Zeus. He can be the killer in me," I said smiling at her.

Without a word she took off her clothes and shifted and

picked her clothes with her mouth and put them by the shed. I decided to do the same. As I put my clothes by hers, I shook my head and went into the woods after her. Zeus got excited and asked to be in control till we got back to the shed. I told him yes and he took off after her.

"Where are you going?" Zeus asked. While in wolf form it's hard to communicate with other wolves that aren't in the same pack. Luckily, both of our wolves can speak broken English.

"Our spot, my love," Noah said.

"We haz a spot?" he asked.

"Da oceans," she smiled.

We got to the ocean in a matter of minutes and sat on the sand letting the waves lap over our paws. I looked at Noah and licked her mouth. She got closer and put her head next to mine. Suddenly, we got pulled into this beautiful garden. I'm not sure what happened, but that place was beautiful.

There were rose bushes, a few hydrangeas, some daisies and my favorite, Hibiscus, and those where just to name a few.

I walked over to the rose bush and bit one and walked over to Noah. Noah took it while I gave her a small nuzzle and licked her mouth as a sign of love. Noah nuzzled me and gave me a small lick back.

I blinked and we were suddenly back at the beach with the water hitting our paws. We looked at the water and then back at each other. I knew we were both confused but Noah moved her head to the left and took off. I shook my head and took off running full speed after her. The sand underneath my paws made me run faster. Zeus could have easily outrun Noah, but I let her wolf have her fun and take the lead.

She thundered ahead, deeper into the woods. I finally caught up to her and found her by an abandoned building. I cocked my head in confusion, but I was willing to follow my mate anywhere. She shifted back into human form and I followed suit.

She let out a giggle and said, "Come on it'll be fun."

"Are you sure?" I asked.

"Yes," she said grabbing my hand and pulled me inside.

We walked inside and entered a similar room that her friend took us to not all that long ago. Once inside, we looked at each other. It was eerie how it looked exactly like the place from the dream. We looked around to see everything was the same from the ceiling to the floor.

"What is this place?" I asked.

"This used to be my grandparents' house. When they passed, my dad built the house that I live in today. I sometimes come out here and think. No one knows about this house except for two people, well three, now. My brother, Lavender and now you. So, don't tell anyone unless it's import," she said looking around.

"I won't, you have my word, but why are we here?" I asked.

"When we got sent here, I thought that maybe there's something that my grandparents left behind for me to find or something. I don't know, I just thought we should come here and see if we could get clarity on what it meant," Claudia said.

"Okay, let's look around. Where do you want to start?" I asked, looking around.

"Here in this room since it's the room that we were sent to. There must be something in here. If it's not in this room, then we will go to others," she said as she started to poke around.

I walked to the other side of the room. I had no idea what I was looking for, but I showed her everything that I thought could be something. There were piles of things on the floor and in the cupboards. It was all old and dusty and it smelled terrible. Nothing I showed her in this room was anything of importance. After looking around for half an hour we decided to split up and each take a different room. I entered the right side of the house and she took the left.

I was about to give up after searching half a dozen rooms until I entered the last one on the right, which looked like it was her grandparents' bedroom.

I found it in a drawer in an old wardrobe. I don't know how I knew that this is what we were looking for, I just did. I took it in my hand and was about to bring it to Claudia when she entered the room.

She saw me cupping it in my hand and said, "You found it! Let's change back to our wolf forms so we can go back to everyone. I don't think walking back naked would be a good idea," she giggled and walked to the busted-out window.

"Let someone touch you, I'll fucking kill 'em. No one gets to fucking touch what's mine," I said with a growl as I walked to the window as well.

"I know, that's why I said to shift back," she said, rolling her eyes.

We shifted back and took off back to the pack house. I held the disc in my month and took off past Noah. I looked back and saw Noah with a big smile on her face. Noah used all her strength and speed to try to catch up to me, but she couldn't. I didn't let her win this time. We passed by the ocean again and I let out a yip in response to the sudden rush of air.

She ran past me at full speed. I shook my head and took off full speed, zooming past her. I slowed down when I saw the shed where we had left our clothes. I shifted back and got dressed before anyone saw me. Noah came running towards me. As she did, she shifted mid run and picked up her clothes and changed as well.

"Hey, put that in your pocket. We don't want anyone to know about the disc, even Paul," Claudia said.

I put the disc in my pocket, and we walked towards everyone. As we made our way towards everyone, Yasmeen walked over to us and wrapped her arms around me. Claudia looked at her and growled as if Noah wanted to come out. I watched as she grabbed Yasmeen's hair and yanked her down to the ground.

"Hey, what the shit?" Yasmeen yelled.

"Get your slutty paws off my mate! If I see you touching him again, I will rip you apart," Claudia said showing her teeth.

"Your mate? He's mine so shut the fuck up, you bitch!" Yasmeen said, trying to not cry.

Claudia didn't respond, I watched as Noah took over and threw Yasmeen across the yard.

"Noah that's enough. I will take it from here. She is in my pack and I will take care out her punishment." I spoke.

"She is in my house! I will kill her!" Noah said.

Before I could move towards Noah, Paul walked over to her and then shifted into his wolf form. I didn't see him take his clothes off before shifted. He placed his paw on her to calm her down.

"Noah, give us Claudia back, please. We need her to come back so we can talk," he told Noah.

She looked at me, her eyes were starting to shift, and I knew Claudia was coming back in control.

"Is she gone? I don't want her anywhere near you Carson. I mean it," Claudia said looking around.

"She will get what's coming to her but she belongs to my pack so I will deal with her later," I told her. I looked to where Yasmeen landed and noticed she was gone.

"Lilly Pad, where did you run off to and who were you with?" Paul asked after he shifted back to his human form. He pulled his shirt back on and pulled up his shorts.

"I was with Carson, I wanted to show him something," Claudia said, looking at Paul.

"I was worried about you, little one. We are all that we have left since Mom and Dad passed," Paul said to her as he wrapped her up in a bear hug.

"I know you do, I'm sorry. I should have told you I was leaving," she said.

I walked away so they could have some space. I wanted to talk to Harper about this disc and see what his take on it was. I walked over to him and saw that he was talking to a tiny little thing with dark brown hair falling straight down her back. Her blue eyes were glittering as she laughed at my brother's stupid jokes. Any girl who wanted to get in my brother's pants always laughed at his corny jokes. I walked over to them to see what she was like and more importantly what they were talking about.

"Hello, I'm Alpha Carson. Who might you be?" I asked, giving her a small smile.

"My name is Mikayla. I'm Claudia's cousin, so if you break her heart or anything of that sort, I will kill you. Do you understand me?" she said looking me up and down.

"Yes, I understand," I laughed. "She must be your mate because she is just like you, little brother," I said giving him a wink.

"Yeah, I think she is. I didn't think I'd find her here of all places," Harper said, rubbing the back of his neck.

"It's okay. I didn't think I'd find one either," I said to him with a smile before turning to her. "Can I speak to my brother really quickly?"

"Of course. I need to check on Claudia anyway," she said.

As she reached Claudia I turned to Harper and pulled out the disc that Claudia and I found at her grandparents' house.

"Have you seen anything like this at Gram's house? It looks like it had a pair," I asked him, flipping it over in my hands.

"I don't remember but we can go back and check. You own the house now so you can come and go whenever you please," Harper said with a shrug, looking at real close.

"Tomorrow, you and I will go search Gram's house. Take a picture before I give this back to Claudia," I told him.

After he took a picture of the disc, I walked back over to Claudia. I placed the disk in her hand discreetly since she didn't want anyone knowing about it. She gave me a smile and mouthed "thank you". I smiled back and gave her a nod. I stood there for a few seconds to take her in, to smell that beautiful, sweet smell of hers. After a while, I gathered my pack up and told everyone goodbye. I had some things to take care of, starting with Yasmeen.

I COULDN'T BELIEVE that I almost kicked that bitch Yasmeen's ass. I was so angry when I saw her hugging on Carson. That was when Noah came out and shit got ugly. Luckily, Paul was there to calm me down. I also couldn't believe how badly I wanted to make love to Carson. Something about him made me want to go crazy. I couldn't put my finger on it, but it was like we were meant to be together and not just being mates, either. It didn't seem like it was that simple.

I needed to do some research on the disc and why our tattoos pulsed and burned. I thought it might be in our family history book. I left the party that was still underway even though Carson's pack left already and headed inside to the library. I needed to be away from everyone for a bit.

I got to the library and started to look for the family history book and family scroll. I was so wrapped up in trying to find them that I didn't hear footsteps behind me. I turned around to see Mikayla, June and Lorren standing in the door away.

"Are you okay?" Mikayla asked.

"Yeah, just trying to find more information on a disc that Carson and I found. Also, our tattoos keep burning and pulsing. I just think that it's more than us being mates, but I don't know what it could be," I said looking down at my feet. I knew I could trust them; I wasn't worried about them telling anyone.

"We can help you if you want," June said as she stepped further into the room.

"Sure, that would be great. I need the family history book, the family scrolls, and the ancient rune book as well as the Romaine history book on Carson's family," I said as I looked around.

"Okay, we can split up and look for each one," Lorren suggested.

"That's a great idea," I said as I made my way to the back of the library.

Mikayla went to the left side of the room, Lorren went to the right and June took the front of the library. We spent hours looking for everything. We even switched places so that there were fresh eyes on everything.

"I think I found the ancient rune book," June said as she wiped dust off an old book.

Everyone walked over to the desk that sat in the middle of the room. She put the old, weathered book down. I carefully opened it to the first page and as I did so, dust filled the air, and a creak came out as it opened. I grabbed the disc and placed it on the desk next to the book. I began to carefully flip the pages until I found one of the runes on the disc.

The main rune was cut in half, but I did my best with what I could see. It looked like it could be either a warrior rune or a ruler rune. Both looked similar but until I found the other half, I wouldn't know which one it was. From what I could tell, it was made from some type of stone and looked like it was from the tenth century. It had a V that was flipped to the left and above it was a line. Below the V shape was a line that was pointed down.

I needed the other piece to know for sure, but at least I knew what it could possibly mean. I closed the book with a piece of paper to mark the runes. I put the disc on the book and put it to the side.

"Okay let's look for the others," I told them.

It didn't take long for Mikayla to find our family history book.

"Hmm, it doesn't have any dust on it. I wonder who took it out recently? I would think it would have dust like the ancient rune book," Lorren said.

"That's what I was thinking," I said.

Mikayla walked over to the desk and placed it beside the ancient rune book. I opened the book to my dad and mom's page where it showed my parents and I also see my brother and Abby. Beside them was Carson and me. I looked up a bit shocked that Carson's name was in it already even though we hadn't marked each other. I looked at the girls and they all had the same look on their face. I turned the page. It read: *Claudia Stonewell destined to mate with Carson Blackmen,*

King of Romaine and Queen of America wolf packs. Royal blood will be alive once more.

"What the hell does that mean?" June said.

"I'm not sure, but let's find his family book to see if it has the same thing," I said.

We kept looking for Carson's family book. Before long, June accidentally tripped over a stack of books that I had been meaning to put away.

"Hey, I found it. It was in this stack of books," she said as she stood up with a thick book in her hands.

We opened it up and flipped through it until we found his family's page. Next to his name was mine and to the left of it was Harper and next to his name was Mikayla. We all looked up and saw Mikayla's face had a smile on it.

"When we had them over, Harper and I found out that we are mates!" she said jumping up and down.

"When were you going to tell us?" Lorren asked.

"I was planning on telling everyone, but Claudia needed our help," Mikayla said as she looked down.

"Congrats, Mikayla. Let's focus on this so we can finish," I said looking at them.

We found the same thing written on the back of the page and I told the girls that we needed to find the family scrolls to get a better understanding. We walked towards the back of the library to the right into a separate room full of scrolls of different things. It was a small room, so we decided not to be spilt up but have two people per side of the room. We pulled out scroll after scroll to find the family name on them. June took out a very old and worn scroll to find that it bore my family's name.

"Hey, look here. It says, "The king of all wolves will be mated to our first female Alpha, Claudia Stonewell. She will then be queen of all wolves. This had been set in time since wolves have been created. They will be the most powerful pack to roam the earth in history. Claudia and Carson were mated before their family was ever made.""

"What does that mean?" she asked.

"I'm not sure but I need to bring this over to Carson to show him. Thank you, loves, for helping me." I smiled at them as I gathered everything and carried it out of the library.

I dialed Carson's number and he picked up on the first ring. "Hello?"

"Hey, it's Claudia. Can I come over? I have some things to show you," I asked as I grabbed a jacket.

"Salut pisoi (hello kitten). Of course, you can come over anytime," he said smiling at every word.

"Awesome, I'll be there soon. Can you send me your address?" I asked as I walk outside.

"Yes, pisoi, I can," he said.

I walked out of my house and over to my car. It was an electric blue 2019 Civic coupe. I started the car and put on my favorite rock station and turned the volume up loud. I typed in Carson's address and started driving.

After a ten-minute drive I turned into the driveway and saw a beautiful log cabin. I got out and was greeted by Harper and a guy with spiked black hair.

"Hey, Harper!" I said as I climbed out of my car.

"Hey, my brother is inside," he said.

"Oh, let me help you with those. I'm Nikko," the guy standing next to Harper said as he grabbed the books from my hands.

"Thank you and nice to meet you. We briefly meet at my house," I said, giving him a small smile.

I followed Harper and Nikko into the house. I was greeted by the rest of the pack. I also saw the bitch that was hugging on Carson. She had a shit eating grin on her face and her blond hair was falling down her back. Her brown eyes sunk into her face and her green lipstick made her look like a hooker. Her outfit wasn't much better than her shitty makeup. She was wearing a red crop top with a choker and bright yellow short shorts with red heels.

"Did you dress in the dark?" I asked, looking her up and down.

"No, Carson likes it when I dress like this," she said, smiling even wider.

"I doubt that. If you excuse me, I have a meeting with my mate," I said smiling at her.

She was about to say something when Carson walked into the room and said, "Pisoi, you look beautiful. Follow me."

I followed Carson to an office where he shut the door and locked it.

"So, what did you have to show me?" he asked as he kissed my forehead.

"I found some interesting things that might explain every-thing." I smiled as I set the books and scroll down on the desk. I first opened the ancient book of runes and showed him what the disc could possibly mean.

"I have a feeling that I have the other part of the disc somewhere," Carson said as he rubbed his chin.

"This is just the beginning," I told him as I closed the book. I grabbed the family books and opened them to our family tree. I then showed him what was written on the back of both. He was quiet, so I decided to show him my family scroll. He still hadn't said anything. I moved to close the scrolls when he grabbed my hand and shook his head.

"I want to show my brother. I think you should call yours so he can see this as well," he said as he handed me his phone.

I grabbed the phone and called Paul, "Hey, can you come to Carson's house? I need to show you something."

Within minutes Harper and Paul were in the room and reading the text from the books and scroll. They were speechless when they finished. I looked around the room to see that all three of them looked like they saw a ghost.

"Are y'all okay?" I asked.

"What? Oh, yeah," Paul said.

I giggled as I closed the books and rolled up the scroll. I handed them to Paul to be brought back to the house when he left.

"You're going to stay?" Paul asked.

"I want to talk to Carson some more. I'll be home later," I said with a smile.

"Okay," he said as he walked out of the office.

I turned around to say something to Carson but before I

could, that bitch Yasmeen snuck in and placed her nasty hands on him. Everything went black. I grabbed her by her hair and dragged her down the hall and to the back door. I opened it with my right hand as my left hand tightened its grip on her hair, I threw her across the yard. I saw her getting up and charge me, but I moved to the left to avoid the hit. I grabbed her by her leg and threw her again and she landed with a thud. I walked over to her and bent down and told her, "Get your nasty ass up and fight me."

She got up and tried to punch me. I couldn't take anymore as I shifted into my wolf. She soon followed suit and shifted as well. I let her get in a few hits before I grabbed her by the throat and pinned her down to the ground waiting for her to submit to me. She continued to growl and move underneath me. I let go of her and kicked her in her side. She began to whimper. I honestly wanted to rip her throat out, but she was not in my pack. Instead, I walked over and stood over her as I let out a growl that made everyone but Carson whimper and bow their heads. She finally submitted to me as her Alpha.

"Oh, you fight like a girl by the way," I said as I shifted back.

9 CLAUDIA

I WALKED AWAY from Yasmeen to Carson and turned back to see blood coming out of her mouth and nose. I could tell it was going to take some time to stop but I was not concerned with her well-being. I let out a laugh and wrapped my arms around his waist.

"Where were we?" I said looking up at him.

"I believe you wanted to talk more on what you found. Let's go inside my office and talk more," he said smiling down at me.

"Yes, sir." I stepped to the side so he can walk ahead of me.

We walked into the office and Carson made sure that the door was locked. I walked over to the sofa that was against the left wall. It was upholstered in black leather and very comfortable. Carson had more than likely spent a few nights on this. I could tell by the way it dipped lower in some parts, as if it was worn in. He walked over and sat next to me on my right side.

"I knew I came from royal blood but never thought that we were meant to be together," he said running his hand through his hair.

"I never knew much about my family 'til Paul was able to get the scrolls and the history book. That explains why every pack's Alpha tries to challenge me. They want to rule. I always thought my dad was crazy when he would make us train non-stop," I said rubbing my right arm.

"I'm here and I'm not letting anyone take our throne. I will protect you through everything." He wrapped his arms around me and kissed the top of my head.

I gave him a smile. "I don't know if we should tell our packs, though."

"I think they deserve to know what's going on. I also think we should combine packs." He gave me a small squeeze.

"Okay, let's have some pack members stay here to watch this side and we can expand into downtown, where you asked me about yesterday," I said looking up into those beautiful eyes.

"I like that. We can have everyone meet us here and we can divide them accordingly," he said, removing his arms and placing his hands in mine.

I gave a small nod. I just wanted to fall asleep in his arms and never leave. I felt so safe in them.

"Do you want to spend the night here?" he asked, reading my mind. "Tomorrow we can have everyone come here and we can share the news. We can also divide the pack into the houses, like you said," Carson said as he kissed the top of my head.

"I'd like that. I just hope everyone doesn't hate me," I said.

"If they do then they will have to deal with me." He wrapped me up tighter.

He let go of me, standing up and reaching out his hand for me to take. I put my hand in his and stood up. He led me out of his office and down the hall. I'm glad that I had Carson's hand showing me where to go because the house was huge. We got to a door that had a sign that read Alpha on it. He opened it and I saw a beautiful room behind it that had a whole wall full of posters. The other wall had a dresser with a tv hanging above it and a small table that sat in the corner with a game system.

I walked over to the table to see that it had two game systems, an Xbox One and a PS4. I turned around to see a California King size bed sitting in the middle of the room with clothes thrown on it.

"Were you planning on folding the clothes or sleeping on top of them?" I giggled.

"Oh, um...you know folding them and then sleeping on top of them," he smiled.

"At least they'd be folded," I said and giggled louder.

He picked up the clothes and put them in the dresser and handed me a shirt to sleep in. I grabbed the shirt and made my way to the bathroom that was connected to the room. I closed the door and got undressed, but before long there is a knock.

"What are you doing, beautiful?" Carson asked as he walked to the bathroom door.

"I need a shower. I smell like that nasty hoe," I said, trying not vomit.

"Can I join you in the shower?" he asked, trying not to laugh.

I walked over to the door and unlocked it. I opened the door and Carson's face lit up as he saw my naked body. I smirked and walked over to the bathtub. I turned on the water and let the hot steam fill the room.

"You look beautiful," Carson said, moving my hair to one side.

"Thank you." I turned around and I saw Carson naked as well.

"Like what you see?" he asked with a huge smile on his face.

"Wait what...? Oh um, nice," I blushed. I didn't wait for a reply. I got in the tub. I heard him laughing as he climbed in after me. He gave me a kiss on the neck where my birth tattoo was, and my knees went weak as I let out a small moan.

"I don't want to mark you until you said so. I will wait until you are ready, but I will rip someone apart if they think they can take you from me," Carson said as he kissed me again and let out a low growl.

"I appreciate that. I do want to try something, though," I said as I felt my cheeks heat up again.

"Yes love, what is it that you want to try?" he asked.

I reached down and grabbed his manhood. I started to play with it and made it hard. My eyes widened as I saw how big he was. I urged Carson to sit on the edge of the tub as I got on my knees and began to lick the tip. Carson began to moan. I then moved to take the top half in my mouth. I twirled my tongue around in different directions. As I continued to do that, Carson began to moan louder and called out my name. I took the whole length of him in my mouth and picked up the pace, going faster and taking all of him in at once.

He wrapped my hair in his fists. "Stay still. I'm going to fuck you in the mouth. I want you to be on your hands and knees now," he said as he stood up and took a step back.

"Yes sir, anything for you master," I said, putting my hands on the bottom of the tub and looking up at him. The warmth from the water and the sight of Carson before me gave me the most heated feeling between my legs.

"Good girl. I love when you call me your master. That is what you are going to call me when we enter this room and the bedroom. Do you understand?" he asked as he pulled my hair making me moan.

"Yes master," I said, looking up at him.

He smiled as he grabbed his penis in his right hand, running his hand along it. He took a few steps towards me. I licked my lips waiting for his lollipop. Suddenly, he put his shaft in my mouth and thrusted it in and out. He started off slow and easy. I continued to twirl my tongue around it. He tightened the grip on my hair and moved faster as he slammed into my mouth.

Barely five minutes of him slamming into my mouth he began to get sloppy and unorganized. I could tell he was getting ready to cum. He finally reached his high and I felt the hot liquid shoot into my mouth. He was about to pull out when I pull him closer and continued to suck him until he was dry. When I was done, I backed up and smiled at him.

"Damn, that had to be the best blow job on the planet," Carson said as he gave me a kiss.

"Thank you, love. Now, let's wash up," I said.

I let the water run down my body as he grabbed the shampoo and put some in his hand. He motioned for me to come to him. I did as I was told as I stood up. He washed my hair and it felt so amazing. His hands were strong and attentive. When he finished, I rinsed it out and grabbed the bodywash. I washed my body, and I could feel his eyes on me, watching my every move.

"Would you like me to wash you up, master?" I asked.

"I would like that. Yes, my beautiful girl." He grabbed his loofah and his body wash.

I took the loofah, and he squeezed some body wash onto it. I washed his lower body and then moved up to his chest and his back. I made sure that I covered his whole body before I rinsed off the loofah. I let him rinse off and then I got back under the water as he climbed out. After a few minutes I did the same and wrapped a towel around my hair and around myself and I turned the shower off. I walked out of the bathroom and into the bedroom to find him lying in the bed with nothing on.

"You like the view, sweetheart?" he asked as he looked me over.

"Do you sleep naked?" I asked as I walked over to the

other side of the bed and let the towel fall. I removed the towel from my hair and discarded that too.

"Yeah, I do," he smiled.

"Another thing we have in common," I said, laying down on my stomach.

"Well, my queen. I need to do something for you. You deserve pleasure as much as I do," he said, pulling me closer to him.

"What would that be my king?" I turned to face him.

"Lay on your back and don't move," he growled.

"Yes, sir," I giggled.

I rolled on my back in the middle of the bed. He slid off the bed and walked around it so he could view me from every angle. He let out a low growl and his eyes went back and forth from emerald to clover green. My eyes followed him, but I didn't move an inch. He climbed back on the bed and kissed my forehead.

"Tell me to stop if I get too rough, okay?" he said in my ear.

"I love it rough. Bring it on, boy," I said with a smile.

10

CARSON

A SMILE SPREAD across my face. I was more than willing to get rough if that's what she wanted. Wait, did she just call me boy? She was going to find out that is not acceptable in my bedroom. I grabbed her by her waist and flipped her over as I smacked her perfectly round little ass. I kissed both cheeks as a thought crossed my mind. I ran my fingers along the crack of her ass.

She started to move under my touch. I smiled as I slipped a finger in her hole. I moved it nice and slow and she started to moan. I picked up the pace as she got louder. I was getting turned on even more. I pulled my finger out and flipped her on her back. I let her catch her breath before I began to kiss her eyes, then her lips and down to her collarbone. I trailed down to her left breast, then her right one. I felt her squirm as I kissed her breasts. I sucked on her right one as I flicked my thumb over her left one.

She went crazy and I smiled. I took her nipple in between my teeth and pulled on it. She let out a moan and grabbed my hair. I kept doing that for a few minutes before I began to do the same on the left. When I decided that she'd had enough I moved down to her sweetness. I flicked my tongue against her clit, and she went wild. I kissed her inner thighs and then moved back to lick her clit again as she started to squirm under me. I grabbed her arms and picked up my head. I shook it to tell her to stop. I put my head back down and started back up again. I decided to draw the alphabet with my tongue.

I went through all of them and backwards until I was sure that letter R was the one that made her body arch. I repeated that a few times and then I moved on to slide a finger into her sweetness. I started off nice and slow like I did when I fingered her ass. She moaned even more, and I could tell that she enjoyed this. I sat up and picked up the pace. I could see her eyes rolling back in her head as she fought her undoing in my hands.

"That's right, cum for me little girl," I said as she covered my fingers with her cum. She found her release and I pulled my figures out.

"More please, I want more!" she begged me to keep going.

"You want me to fuck you?" I asked kissing her sweetness as I cleaned her up with my tongue.

"Yes, please. I want you, now!" she said through deep breaths.

"With great pleasure but remember to tell me if I get too rough," I said as I moved in and out of her with my tongue.

"O…okay," was all that she managed to say.

I let out a laugh and stood up to get my penis ready. When it was nice and hard, I flipped her over to her stomach and positioned her so that her ass was in the air. Wolves are different than humans, we can have anal without lube. We also can get rough and live for the rough shit. I grabbed her hair in my right hand and with my left hand I placed it on her hip. I didn't even give her a chance to think about it. I slammed into her nice little ass. She let out a yell of surprise but after a few pumps she began to moan and asked me to go faster which I did with pleasure.

I didn't stay in long. I didn't want to spend the whole time just on her ass. I pulled out and slam into her sweet pussy and she screamed my name and asked me to go faster and harder. Again, I did without her having to ask twice. I pulled out after a few pumps and flipped her on her back and before she could get comfortable, I slammed into her.

Being inside of her was amazing. She fit around me tightly. I could fuck her all damn day. Most girls couldn't take all of me, a lot of them would have told me to stop by now but she just kept telling me to keep going. I had both hands on the headboard as I slammed harder into her. I took my left hand and started to choke her, and she started to shake like she was going to climax.

"Oh no you don't." I slowed down.

"Please master, please. I've been a good girl," she begged as she wriggled under me.

"Stop moving and I will let you cum," I said fighting for control with Zeus.

"Yes master." She stopped moving.

I slammed into her and continued to choke her as I could feel both of us coming undone. As we both came, I felt my neck burn then a rush of euphoria. We both let out a howl of pleasure as I rolled off and pulled her closer to me.

"I'm sorry. I couldn't wait any longer. Noah took over and marked you," Claudia said looking away.

"Hey, I'm not mad at you. I'm glad you did because I was fighting Zeus for control," I said making her look at me.

"I have to say for my first time it was the best night ever," she said cuddling up to me.

"I still can't believe that you were a virgin. That blow job was definitely the best I ever had," I said wrapping my arms around her.

"Believe it," she said, letting out a yawn.

"If you say so, my love," I said kissing the top of her head.

"Mm," she said as she fell asleep.

I let out a chuckle and closed my eyes after her. I fell into a deep sleep and I got pulled into a dream where my mom and dad were standing in the family garden.

They were talking but I couldn't hear them. I moved closer to them to hear what they were saying. As I did, I saw my younger self running up to my parents. I stopped and hid in a nearby rose bush. I remembered this day; it was the day right before they got killed by rouge wolves and the pack that I am still after. I wanted to go get ice cream at the local parlor.

Harper and I didn't fight for a whole week. I wished I could give them a hug but all too soon I was pulled away.

I woke up and Claudia was still asleep, so I kissed her head and decided to make her breakfast in bed. I walked into the kitchen and started making food for everyone. I cooked up bacon, sausage, ham, pancakes, waffles, grits, oatmeal, and eggs. I popped some toast in the toaster and brewed some coffee for everyone. I poured some orange juice in a cup. I put a little bit of everything on a tray and started to walk back to the bedroom when I saw Yasmeen coming my way.

"Hello sexy," she said, looking around.

"Hello Yasmeen. I am your Alpha. You will call me that, or I will give out your punishment," I said walking past her.

"Wait, what? I thought we were mates. Did she mark you?" She moved to grab my arm.

"Claudia is my mate and your Luna. Remember that, because next time I will let her kill you," I said walking to the bedroom.

I walked in to see that Claudia was still asleep. I put the tray down on the table next to the bed. I sat on the edge of the bed and gently shook her awake.

"Good morning beautiful. I made breakfast for you," I said, giving her a smile.

"Good morning. You made me food? Thank you." She sat up.

"How are you feeling?" I asked her as I grabbed the tray and placed it on the bed.

"A bit sore but I'm okay. Food please." She reached out to grab the coffee cup.

I let out a low chuckle and handed her the plate and a fork, "Here you go, love. Eat and then I'll run you a bath."

"Thank you. I could use a bath after last night," she said as she shoved a piece of pancake and sausage in her mouth.

We sat on the bed, ate breakfast and talked about how we were going to break the news to everyone. She asked for more food which I was happy to refill for her. We both ate our second helpings and I walked to the kitchen to put the dishes in the sink. I grabbed the bubble bath soap and bath salts from the girl's bathroom. I walked into the bedroom and she was sitting on the bed drawing.

"You draw?" I ask her, walking into the bathroom.

"Oh yeah, for fun. I'm not that good," she said.

"Let me see and I'll be the judge of that." I walked back over to her.

"Is that me?" I asked looking at the paper.

"Yeah. I draw people more than anything," she said as she closed it.

"That's really good. Now let's get you into that bath that I promised you," I said holding out my hand.

She grabbed it and I led her to the tub. I grabbed the bubble bath and squeezed it into the tub as bubbles started to appear. I opened a small packet of bath salts and poured them in the tub as well. She stepped in and gently sat down and smiled but winced a bit as she got settled in the tub.

"How does it feel?" I asked her.

"A lot better. I think I'm going to soak for a bit," she said as she took a deep breath.

"Okay that's fine. I'll be in my office. You can wear one of my shirts and a pair of sweatpants if you want," I said, giving her a kiss. Before I walked out of the bathroom, I placed a towel next to the tub.

"Okay, thank you," she called after me.

CARSON

I WALKED out of the bathroom and to the dresser. I grabbed my favorite band shirt, Hollywood Undead, and I pulled it over my head. Grabbing a pair of ripped jeans, I slipped my belt through the loops and fastened it. I slipped on my black Vans and headed out to my office down the hall.

I mind linked with Harper, "Hey grab Nikko and Ryden and meet me in the office. I have some things that I need to talk about."

"Okay, I'll go grab them and be there soon," he said back.

I turned on my desktop and opened my emails so I could check them while I waited on the guys, knowing it could be a little bit before they showed up. I saw that I had a few spam emails and a few ads in my inbox, but nothing important. I was just getting ready to turn off the computer when the boys knocked on the door.

"Who is it?" I asked looking up from the screen.

"It's me, Alpha," said Nikko.

"Come in," I said turning off the computer.

The guys walked in and sat on the sofa against the far wall. I looked at all of them and saw that they finally don't have bags under their eyes.

"So, I marked Claudia last night. We also want to split the packs between the houses," I said running my hands through my hair.

"Wait, what?" Nikko asked.

"We had sex and marked each other," I said bluntly.

"No, the other part. We heard you guys last night. We know about the sex and marking," Ryden smirked.

"Oh right. We were talking about splitting the packs between the two houses," I said and shrugged my shoulders.

"Here's an idea, you can build one big pack house in the middle of the land," Nikko said looking at all of us.

"That's not a bad idea. I'll run that by Claudia. She'll probably want to keep her pack house but this one doesn't mean anything to me," I said looking at the guys.

We heard a knock on the door. "Who is it?" I asked, a bit confused.

"It's me, Claudia," she said sweetly.

"Come in, love," I said with a smile.

She walked in wearing my Ice Nine Kills shirt and my navy and red sweatpants. Her feet were bare, and her hair pulled up into a messy bun. She had no makeup on and looked beautiful. I couldn't believe she's my mate and that I get to spend the rest of my life with her.

"Carson did you hear me?" she asked.

"What? No, sorry love. What was it?" I said rubbing the back of my neck.

"I asked if you want to talk about what we are going to do about the packs," she repeated.

"Oh, Nikko was saying something about that. Nikko why don't you tell Claudia what you suggested," I said stepping back letting Nikko take over.

"Well, I was thinking that maybe you both can build a house in the middle of the land. I understand if you don't want to do that, or you can add on to your pack house since it is bigger than this one," Nikko said a bit shyly.

"Actually, adding on to my house isn't a bad idea but what would you do with this one?" she asked looking at me.

"I don't know, tear it down. It doesn't mean much to me, but I know yours does," I said shrugging my shoulders.

"Are you sure?" she asked looking at me then at the guys.

"Yes, love, I am. While you are here, I want to ask you if you know the pack in the Midwest?" I needed all the help I could get with the pack that I was hunting.

"Yes, the Alpha is my brother's best friend. I can see if he can make a trip down here." She grabbed her phone from my pants pocket.

"Thank you, love. Oh, hey guys, have you found your mates yet?" I asked, turning to them.

"Uh… maybe…" Ryden said while Nikko nodded.

I chuckled and shook my head, "So, I take that as a yes. Who are they? Whose pack are they from?" I asked knowingly.

"Claudia's pack," they all said at the same time.

I now felt better that I didn't have to break any new wolves in. I hated it when I had to show newbies how I ran things.

"What are their names?" I asked looking up at them.

"Mine is Mikayla. She's a wild one. You met her already," Harper shrugged.

"Mine is June," Nikko said as he looked away.

"Mine is that pink goddess, Lorren," Ryden said.

"I'm happy for all of you guys," I said.

There was a knock on the door and then it opened. "Alpha, we have a problem. Yasmeen just got attacked," Jarrod told me with a horrid look on his face.

I looked at everyone in the room and we ran out of my office without hesitation and into the back yard. We found Yasmeen covered in blood and barely hanging on. Willow came over and tried to stop the blood, but it was no use. She was bleeding too much. I watched the life drain from her body as she went still.

I looked up and I saw Claudia take off running into the woods in her wolf form. I told everyone to leave Yasmeen's body where it was and I took off after her, disrobing my clothes before I shifted. I saw that she had done the same thing before she took off. Zeus began to talk in Romanian. It's much easier to communicate for him than English and thank God that Noah can understand him.

"Pisoi unde esti (kitten where are you)?" Zeus asked. Now that we were marked, we were able to mind-link which made things much easier.

"Finding the wolf that did this," Noah said.

"Ai vazut cine facut asta (you saw who did this)?" I asked.

"Yes, now shh. I can hear something in the trees on the right," Noah growled.

"Sa mergem (let's go)." I took off towards the right where the noises were coming from.

Noah jumped over me and ran towards the noise. I looked over and saw that she had a jet-black wolf pegged down. I shifted back and mind-linked Harper to meet us with our clothes as I placed my left hand on her and told her to shift back. She did, still holding the wolf in her hand and it shifted back to reveal a male with brown hair and blue eyes.

"What is your name?" I asked him.

"Why do you care?" the stranger said.

"What is your name!" Claudia asked, shaking him.

"Eben. I'm from the Snow Hill pack," he said.

Harper walked up with clothes in his hand. "Do you want me to put him in the cells?" he asked as he handed us our clothes.

"No, I want to fight him. Bring him to the yard and call my pack, please," Claudia said.

"Alpha is that okay?" Harper asked looking at me.

"Yes, she is also your Alpha now. Call Paul and tell him to bring everyone here," I said pulling my shoes on.

"Yes, Alpha." He took off running, dragging Eben with him.

I looked over to Claudia and saw that she was fuming with rage.

"Are you okay?" I asked, walking over and kissing head.

"No. The Alpha that runs Snow Hill is the one that killed my dad," she said as she nuzzled up to me.

"He killed my parents, also." I wrapped my arms around her.

"Let's get going. I need to call a friend of mine." She looked up at me.

We took off running towards the house. Now I wanted to kill him more than ever. I hated seeing her hurt. I hated that he killed a member of my pack. When we got to the house, we saw her pack waiting for us. I saw how everyone was scared too. Claudia walked away towards the house, on her phone.

12 CLAUDIA

I WALKED AWAY from everyone so I could call Ashton. He picked up on the first ring. "Hey, it's Claudia. My mate and I need your help. Can you come down for a few days? I'm going to call the River Falls pack, too."

"Yeah, I can come down. Millie will want to come to see you guys," he said.

"Thank you. I would love to see her!" I said relieved that he agreed to come.

"Give me an hour and I'll be there. Did anything happen?" he asked.

"A wolf from my mate's pack was attacked and died. I ran down the wolf that did it," I said looking back at everyone.

"Okay, leave the body there. I'm getting into the car now. I will try and get there as fast as I can," he said to me as I heard him start his truck.

"Okay be careful. See you when you get here," I said before I hang up.

I walked back to the group and bent down to see Yasmeen's lifeless body. I wondered what made the wolf attack her and not anyone else. As I examined her body, I saw a piece of paper. I took it out of her hands.

"What is that?" Paul asked me.

"I'm not sure but we're about to find out." I unfolded it and smoothed it out.

"It says, "I know what power y'all have and that power will be mine.""

I looked up to see Carson's eyes full of fury.

"Paul, can you call River Falls pack for me? I have to calm Carson," I asked him.

"Yeah, don't worry. Go take care of your mate," he said, nodding his head.

I walked over to Carson and Harper.

"You need to calm down. We won't let anything happen to Claudia. You have my word, brother," Harper said to Carson.

"Hey, we are going to be okay. We will fight this together, side by side," I said putting my hands on his arms.

"Thank you. I just hate seeing you so broken and hurt," he confided to me.

I wrapped my arms around him and said, "I hate seeing you so scared and helpless. I love you too much to see you like this."

I grimaced a little because I realized this is the first time saying those words to him, but then I relaxed when I realized that I meant them. I loved Carson. We had only met a few days ago, but this was how mating worked. When you found that special one, love came easily and fast and according to the research I did, we were destined to be more than just mates.

"I love you too, pisoi," he said as he kissed me.

I smiled from ear to ear. I knew that with him by my side we were unstoppable. I didn't want anything to happen to him or anyone else in the pack. I needed to call one more person. He was an Alpha of a small pack, but they would be willing to help us out until this whole thing blew over. Now that I knew that someone was out to get us, I would need all the help I could get.

"I need to call one more pack from Canada. I will be right back. Will you be okay?" I asked breaking away and taking my phone out of my pocket again.

"Yes, love. Go ahead and make your call." He gave my hand a squeeze.

I gave him a nod and called my friend, Sam. "Hey, I have a question for you."

"Yeah, what is it?" he asked.

"I need your help. One of my mate's pack members was murdered by someone from the Snow Hill pack," I told him.

"Wait, didn't that Alpha kill your dad?" Sam asked.

"Yeah, that's what the evidence showed. Can you come down?" I said pleadingly.

"Of course, I should be there by tomorrow," he said.

"Thank you," I said as I ended the call.

I turned to see that Ashton and his mate, Millie, were here sooner than I thought. I could see Ashton leaning over the body with Carson, Paul, and Harper. I walked over to see what he'd found. I could see he had her on her right side examining her back.

"Have you found anything yet?" I asked.

"Yes, there must have been a fight before he killed her. There's some marks on her back that look like scratch marks," Ashton said as he pulled up her shirt.

"At least she put up a fight, but why go after her?" Paul asked out loud.

"Her and Carson use to fuck, and everyone knew about it," Harper said.

"Thanks, let's tell everyone who I had sex with," Carson said, rolling his eyes.

I let out a giggle. "She was jealous of Carson and I being mates, so maybe she went out looking for a fight?" I said shrugging my shoulders.

"It could be that Snow Hill is trying to kill the people that they think are close to you," Ashton suggested.

"That makes senses, actually," I said as I stood up and took a step back.

"I want to put a stop to this before someone else gets hurt or worse, killed. We will move everyone to your house, and I will be waiting for them here," Carson said as he stood up and investigated the woods.

"I won't let you stay here alone. I'm staying with you," I said, raising my voice.

"I have an idea. How about Carson, Ashton, Sam, Harper, Paul and you can stay here, and Marco and Nikko can manage everyone at your pack house, Claudia," Millie spoke up for the first time.

"We can do that," Marco and Nikko agreed.

"I like the idea. I like a good fight," Sam said as he walked up and looked at Yasmeen's body.

"How did you get here so fast? Did you fly?" I asked a bit puzzled.

"No, I was actually down here when you called. Had some business here. I'm not a damn bat." Sam said a bit hurt by my question.

I thought about Carson's issues with the Light Side pack. I wanted to get to the bottom of that and see if it had anything to do with Waylon, because I knew that pack had had some issues with him in the past. Waylon was a family friend and he had around a lot after my parents died, but we hadn't seen him in a long time. He was always nagging at the back of my mind though, and it seemed like it was a good time to try and find him, although I wasn't sure why. I always had the feeling that he knew more about my parents' deaths than he had led on. I grabbed my phone and called the Light Side pack's Alpha, James.

"Hello, Alpha James?" I asked.

"Yes?" he replied.

"How are you doing?" I asked him.

"Doing fine. Trying to get Alpha Waylon off my back," he said to me.

"Do you mind coming by with your pack? I have a few others here that want to help put an end to your issues with Waylon."

"Give me a few minutes and my pack and I will be on our way," he said before he hung up the phone.

13

CLAUDIA

ASHTON, Paul, Sam, Harper, Carson, and I all sat around the living room in silence. Paul grabbed the TV remote and turned it on to the news. We watched all the news until it was over in complete silence.

"Anyone hungry?" I asked.

"Yeah," Paul said and everyone else nodded.

"Okay, I'll cook us something to eat. What do you guys want?" I asked, getting up and walking to the kitchen.

"What about fried chicken?" Carson asked.

"Yeah, that sounds great," Paul said.

"I can do that. It'll be a little bit before it is ready," I tell them.

I took all the ingredients out of the cupboards and the refrigerator. I set them down and grabbed a bowl so I could pour the buttermilk in it, along with eggs and flour. I seasoned everything and waited for oil to come to the right temperature to fry. I dredge the chicken and worked on making cornbread waffles. I placed the chicken in the oil and started making the waffles. I cleaned up the kitchen as everything cooked. I loved cooking, it helped relax me after a long day, and this, in fact, had been a long day.

I pulled the last pieces of chicken out of the frying pan and took the last waffle out of the waffle maker. I sat everything out on the table and admired my work.

"Boys the food is ready, come eat!" I yelled from the kitchen.

I heard footsteps as they all headed into the kitchen. One by one, they grabbed plates and piled them with food. I grabbed myself a helping once they were done and digging into their plates. I sat down with them and started to eat when we heard the cell monitor go off. We looked over at the screen that was the live feed from the cell to see that Eben was trying to get out.

"Should I bring him some food?" I asked.

"No, he doesn't need food," Carson said.

"He looks hungry and maybe I can get him to talk," I said to them.

"Fine, but I will be watching you like a hawk, or I should say a wolf looking after his mate," Carson said through a growl.

I grabbed a paper plate and a piece of chicken and a waffle with a cup of syrup. I grabbed a plastic fork and knife and made my way to the cells.

When I got to the cells, I could hear Eben talking to someone or something. I made my way to his cell and found him alone talking to himself.

"I brought you some food. I hope you like it," I said pushing the plate and cup through the bars.

"Why are you giving me food?" he asked.

"I figured you must be hungry," I said looking at him.

"I am…thank you." He hesitantly grabbed the plate and cup.

"Who were you talking to when I came in?" I asked as I sat down on the bench outside of the cell.

"Oh, you heard that?" Eben asked, running his hands through his hair.

"Yeah, but I didn't hear everything." I shrugged my shoulders.

"My mate. She wants to get out of the pack we are in and join a different one," he said looking down.

"Why?"

"She said that the Alpha wants to kill every pack in the U.S., and she doesn't want to be a part of it. She wants me to surrender to you all so that I can join your pack. That way, she can come join as well," he said in between bites.

"Why would we let you in our pack after what you did?" I asked getting up.

"It wasn't like that. I know it looks bad, but it wasn't that simple," he said, hanging his head.

"Tell me what happened," I demanded.

"I was just in the woods, minding my business when she came along looking for a fight. She said that if I killed her, it would make Carson, her Alpha, go to war and if I didn't kill her, she was going to go to my Alpha and ask him to kill you. I was mind-linked to my Alpha and he ordered me to kill her." He put his head in his hands. "I couldn't disobey my Alpha, so I did what I was told."

"Thank you for telling me the truth. I will let everyone know what you just told me, and I will be back soon." I gave him a small smile.

I made my way back up to the living room and I found the guys standing around the monitor. I let out a small cough to let them now that I was back.

"We have to let him and his mate join. Yasmeen was a traitor and was going to have us killed," I said, as I fought to keep Noah at bay.

"Fine, but I will go down and talk to him tomorrow. For now, we need to make a plan for all of these attacks," Carson said.

"It might be a little late for that, Carson," Ashton said as he pointed out the back window.

I looked out to see the back yard filled with wolves and there aren't any from our pack. I ran to the cells and I told Eben that he and his mate could be in the pack.

"Thank you. My mate will be so pleased," he said.

"You're welcome but right now, there is an attack on us, and I think it might be your former pack. We need your help," I rushed to say.

He nodded and we ran into the living room to find Sam in mid fight with a black wolf.

"I have to find my mate," Eben said as he ran into the back yard.

I ran out after him so that I could fight with the others. I ran over to a brown wolf trying to attack Paul. I shifted into my wolf and let Noah take over the fighting. I let out a protective growl and stood in front of Paul. I grabbed the brown wolf by the throat and ripped it out and then I ran over to a gray wolf who was just watching the scene unfold. As soon as it saw us coming it ran into the woods. I looked over at Carson and noticed that he saw it too. We took off after the gray wolf and cornered it in the woods. I shifted back to my human form and so did Carson.

"Shift! That's an order!" Carson yelled at the gray wolf.

It shifted to reveal the Alpha of Snow Hill, Reese. "We will win this war," he said with a sneer.

"What war? There is no war," I spat back at him.

"The war of all wars. The war of power," Reese said.

"Who is ordering this?" Carson asked.

"The old bat, Waylon from the Winterstone pack. He wants the throne for himself and if packs won't join him, then he kills them," Reese said getting up.

"We can offer you a pardon if you join us," I tell him, thinking fast.

"We need a place to stay," Reese said.

"Here is fine," I told him, looking over at Carson.

Carson walked away to tell the guys to stop fighting. I looked back at Reese and saw that he was doing the same with his pack. We walked back to the house to see only three dead and six injured. Reese saw who was dead and shook his head.

"I'm not going to lie, the three that are dead, I won't miss them. Can we get the injured inside and get them healed?" Reese asked us, looking around.

"Of course. I have a few pack members that are healers. I can call them to come over," I said to him.

"Thank you. I owe you both," he said to us.

I gave him a small smile and grabbed my cell. "Hey, I need everyone here. We have a few injured and we have some news about a war that has started," I said to Marco.

"We'll be there in three," Marco responded and hung up.

I turned back around to see everyone inside, all but Carson. I walked over to see if he was okay.

"Hey, are you okay?" I asked him.

"Yeah, but if Waylon is behind all the killings then we need to get everyone on our side. We need to grab everyone that we know to fight this," Carson said looking into the woods.

"We will," I said resting my head on his arm.

We stood there for what felt like a few hours, but it was only a few minutes. I grabbed his arm and pulled him towards the house. We went to the back door and saw Sam and Ashton both on their phones. I opened the door and walked inside. Everyone was sitting around the living room.

"Okay everyone, Waylon is calling for war. I always had the nagging suspicion that he was more foe than friend, and this tells me I know that I was right. Reese is joining the war on our side. His pack will be staying here along with Sam's and Ashton's packs. If it is too crowded here, then I will have a pack stay at the main house," I said looking around.

"What about us?" Willow asked.

"You are a part of mine. Carson is my mate which means his pack is my pack, vice versa. You will be moving into my pack house which is the main house. Go grab your things and move them. I have more than enough room for everyone," I told them.

Ashton walked up to Carson and me. "My pack is on their way."

"Mine as well," Sam chimed in.

I looked at Sam and Ashton, I gave them a smile and walked over to Mikayla where she was tending a wolf who had a cut on his leg. She looked up to see me looking at the cut. I grabbed her some wraps and I gave the wolf a smile. I walked to Lavender who was healing two other wolves. I couldn't see how bad they were, but I knew they were in good hands. I looked over to my left and saw that Bleu, June, and Lorren were taking care of some other wolves and Abby was taking notes on the injuries. Looking around, I realized that we had won this fight, but the war was just beginning.

14

CARSON

I LOOKED AROUND and saw Claudia's pack tending the wounded. I noticed that my pack was helping the ones that had minor injuries. I looked at Claudia and saw her walking around to the wounded and helping. I couldn't quite believe that Waylon was behind the attacks. He had been my father's best friend for years. He was always there for my dad when he had needed him.

I couldn't understand why he was doing this, but if he wanted a war then he would get a war. The real question was, why did he want us dead? I'd build an army if he wanted a damn war and I would not allow anyone else to die because he wanted power. I'd be damned if he thought I would let him kill Claudia or worse, mark her so she was his. The fact that a wolf can try to remark someone else's mate drives me crazy. I wish it can never happen, but it happens more than we would think. I would not let him touch her in any way.

I needed to get out of here before I snapped. There was

too much tension building in that house, and I needed out. I walked to the wood line and took off. I heard someone coming up behind me and I turned around and saw Claudia running to me.

"What's going on?" she asked.

"I just need to clear my head, that's all," I told her.

"Why are you lying to me? I know something is going on, I feel it," she said, looking at me while keeping the pace.

"Waylon is what's wrong. He was always there for my dad so I can't understand why he wants this war," I said, as I fought hard not to shift.

"He was also my dad's best friend. I never liked him. I always had my suspicions that he was behind the attack on my family. I want him dead," she said, somehow calming me down.

"Do you think he killed my father, too?" I asked.

"It's possible. I don't really know anything, it's just a suspicion," she said.

"We are going to need more than just us, Sam and Ashton. I know a pack that owes me a favor. With his pack, we can take on Waylon," I told her as we stopped in front of a house.

It was made of stone and the two-story home was beautiful. All the windows were blown out and the front and back doors looked like they were about to fall over. The basement doors had been ripped from the hinges and thrown down on the grass. The garden hadn't been kept up in years. The weeds were growing all over the place. The big oak tree, still growing tall and strong as ever with the branches hanging down a bit lower than I had remembered, but still beautiful.

"Why are we here?" She looked around.

"It's my Gram's old house that we used to live in," I said as I looked around.

"Hey, I just thought of something. We are still missing that other piece of stone rune. Why don't we look in the house to see if we can find it and figure out what it does?" she said, looking at me with fire in those beautiful purple eyes of hers.

"Yeah, maybe it will help us with the war," I said, bringing her into a hug.

She giggled and tried to wiggle out of my embrace. I pulled her tighter. I didn't want to let go, but I did so we could find the other half of the rune stone. I didn't let her out of my sight, though. We looked outside first. We looked in bushes and in the tall grass and we even dug in the garden to see if it was put there but we came up with nothing.

We made our way inside the house to the front room. I looked at the TV while she looked at the furniture but there was nothing. We moved into the next room, which was the dining room. I investigated the cupboard with the dishes while she looked on the table but still, we found nothing. I was getting frustrated that we weren't finding anything.

We made our way to my mom and dad's room. I looked in the dressers and side table. Claudia looked in the closet and on the bed. I finally came across what we were looking for.

"Is this the stone rune that goes with your piece?" I asked her as she turned around.

"Yeah, that's it. Let's take it back to the house and put it together and see if it does anything." She looked at it closer and took a step back to make her way to the door.

I followed her out of the house and to the yard. I looked at her to see that the look on her face said it all. She took off running back towards the pack house. I shook my head and took off behind her. This woman was going to the death of me. I took a short cut and made it back before she did and let everyone know what we found. She made it back and when she did, Ashton's pack and Sam's pack had already arrived. I looked around and realized that we were going to need some more wolves.

I called my friend Wen. "Hey buddy, can I ask you favor? I need your pack to come help me and my mate fight."

I got the yes from him and hung up the phone as I walked over to Claudia and overheard her telling her friend, Mikayla, to go get the other piece. Her friend nodded her head and walked to a 1986 Mercedes-Benz 560SL and got in with Harper and drove off.

15

MIKAYLA AND HARPER came back with the other piece after only a few minutes. It was nice that our houses were so close together. As we moved to put them together, Wen knocked on the door with his pack. Harper got up and walked to the door to let Wen and his pack in. Wen walked over and looked at the stone runes and cocked his head but said nothing.

"What is it?" I asked him.

"They look like something my great grandfather told me about. I'm sure he was making things up. Please go on to what you were going to do," Wen said.

Before we could continue, another knock came from the door. Paul got up this time to see who it is. Alpha James and his pack walked into the house and stood by Sam. Claudia grabbed her piece before there could be any more disruptions and I did the same. We counted to three and slid them together.

What happened next was something that I never thought

would happen. I felt myself fall to the floor and slipped into a dark sleep. I saw Claudia do the same just before my eyes closed.

We were thrown into a castle that I had never been in or seen before.

We looked at each other and then looked in front of us to see her friend, Lavender, there to guide us to where we needed to go. She waved her hand to signal us to follow her. I grabbed Claudia's hand and followed Lavender. She led us into a grand hall with a throne and people standing around the room. I looked at Claudia to see her with the same puzzled look on her face as I had.

We made our way to the front and found that my great-great grandfather and grandmother were seated on the thrones and that my great grandfather was standing next to them. In front of them was a beautiful woman with long flaming red hair, like Claudia's. She had fair skin and was in a green dress with gold trim. I couldn't make out her face and eyes because she was facing away from me and towards the throne.

I looked over to check on Claudia to see she was looking at the young beautiful woman that looked like her. She turned her head and looked at my great grandfather just as we heard a male voice coming from beside the young woman. It was coming from a hooded man.

"Are you okay?" I whispered in her ear.

"Yes, but what is my great grandmother doing here? Who are those people sitting on the thrones?" she asked looking at me.

"Those are my family and as for your great grandmother, I'm not sure, pisoi." I squeezed her hand.

We continued to watch the scene play out in front of us. The hooded man stood up and grabbed Claudia's great grandmother by the upper arm and threw her at the feet of my great-great-grandfather.

"She means nothing to me anymore. This slave is not worth my time," the male voice said.

"Do not throw a woman to the ground! She is more than a slave," my great grandfather said grabbing her and walking away from the room. I looked at Claudia and saw tears running down her face. I squeezed her hand and looked to see Lavender waving at us to follow her and my great grandfather.

We walked down a hallway into a bed chamber. The bed chamber was beautiful. There was a four-poster bed with dark emerald and gold trim.

The curtains were the same color as the bedding. There was a wall length portrait of my great grandfather on the opposite wall of the wardrobe.

Next to the window was a door. I looked and saw my great grandfather lead Claudia's great grandmother to the door.

"It's okay. I'm not going to hurt you. I just want to help you. My servant will help you. You may stay in this room if you want. I will be in here. My name is Novak," he said as he opened the door.

"T--thank Y--you. My name is Evangeline. I will be glad to stay in this room," she said.

We got pulled into a different time period, both Novak and Evangeline appeared happy and there were two other people with them. I knew one was my great grandmother and the other must be Claudia's great grandfather.

"My sweet Gwendolyn watch out! Evangeline is right behind you!" Novak called out.

"Oh, it's okay. She needs to move anyway," the other man said.

"Oh, Fredrick that's not nice," Evangeline said.

"Well that will teach you to stay out of the way, now won't it? Fredrick teased.

They continued to play and laugh, they looked happy. We were pulled into yet another time period. This time it was when her great grandmother was younger. She looked like she was starving and underweight. I looked at Claudia and saw her eyes were big, but she was silent. I looked back to see the hooded male come into the room and let her out. She looked grateful.

"You run away, and I will sell you, do you understand me?" he said, grabbing her by the arm.

"Y--yes s--sir." Evangeline said, shaking her head.

"Good girl. You will shift and then I will make love to you. Is this clear?" he said.

"Yes sir," she said.

He walked her out to the woods and took a step back. His guards shifted with her and took off. We followed her as she ran through the woods. She managed to outrun his guards and towards the castle. She made her way to an exceptionally large solid black wolf that was walking along the walls of the castle. It stopped and shifted into my great grandfather, Novak.

She shifted back to her human form and wrapped her arms around him,

"I'm sorry but I need your help, sir," she said through tears.

"What is it? I can help you," Novak said, holding her.

"I got kidnaped and I am now a slave to an old man that won't let me go," she said, still crying.

"What is his name? I can talk to my father," he said, pulling her in tight.

"His name is German. He lives just on the other side of the woods to the left," Evangeline said.

We both looked at each other. German is Waylon's relative. We both seemed to know this bit of information.

"Okay, I will let my father know. You should go back before he starts looking for you," Novak said.

"T--thank you!" She ran to the woods and shifted back.

We got pushed out and I woke up on the floor. I got up to see Claudia getting up as well. I looked around and saw Lavender getting out of the chair next to the sofa. I also saw that everyone was looking at us with confused looks on their faces.

"What was all of that?" Harper asked looking at Claudia and me.

"I think it was flashbacks of our great grandfather and great grandmother? But I don't know what it all means," Claudia said.

"I might. Do you have your family scrolls with you?" I asked her.

"Yes, I also have my family's history book," she told me as she pointed out both sitting on a table.

I pulled out my scroll and family history book and set it out on the table next to the rune. I opened the scroll and the book to the page about my great grandfather Novak. I looked at the book to see the name Gwendolyn next to his name. She opened the book to her great grandmother Evangeline and saw that the name Fredrick was next to hers. The scrolls begin to form a type of language that I had learned a long time ago.

It said, "The one who is the saver becomes the saved."

We looked at each other and our tattoos began to pulse, and I began to feel like I was on fire. I noticed that Claudia looked to be feeling the same thing. We ran outside and the intense heat made us take off our clothes and shift into our wolf forms. We each let out a howl and then shifted back again. Claudia ran to me and crushed her lips on mine. I wrapped my arms around her as I deepened the kiss. I picked her up and took her back into the house. I wanted to fuck her so bad; I could tell that she wanted to do the same.

16

CLAUDIA

MY BODY FELT like it was on fire and I wanted Carson inside of me so damn bad. He picked me up and carried me inside and up to his room, ignoring everyone else in the house. He laid me on the bed, and we continued to kiss. I felt Noah at the surface, waiting to fuck him. I didn't want to let her out, but I didn't think I could hold her off much longer. I saw that Carson was having the same problem with Zeus.

I grabbed his arm and pulled him to me. I couldn't hold her back anymore, so I let Noah out and I realized that Carson did the same with Zeus. He moved from my lips to my collarbone and then to my neck. He nipped my neck and I let out a moan as he moved back down to my left breast and started to suck on it.

I moaned and called out his name and he moved to the right and then to my stomach. He kept kissing, moving to my left inner thigh and then to my right inner thigh. I was about to go crazy and I started to moan louder which made him start to eat me out. He began to flick his tongue back and forth as he slid his fingers inside me and began to go in and out as he moved his tongue around.

I moaned louder, knowing that my climax was about to come. He didn't seem to mind because he kept going faster. I grabbed the headboard and arched my back as my climax got closer. I screamed out his name and he kissed my thighs.

"Cum for me, pisoi. Let me feel you cum all over my fingers," he said, going faster.

My climax finally crescendo, and I couldn't even catch my breath before he shoved his manhood in my mouth. I began to suck him. He let out a moan and leaned his head back. I was sucking him for a few minutes before he took it out of my mouth and gave me a kiss. He then shoved all of it inside of me and he began to go in and out as I dug my nails into his back.

I let out a moan as he thrusted faster and harder. I was losing myself and I didn't even care. He pulled out and flipped me over onto my stomach. I got on my knees and put my face in the bed. He slammed into my ass and went deeper than I had ever felt before. I let out a moan and grabbed the bed sheets.

"You like this, pisoi?" he asked.

"Yes, master. YES!" I let out a scream.

"That's my girl," he said as he went faster.

He slipped out and slipped in to hit my sweet spot again and he didn't miss a beat. He continued the pace as he grabbed my hair. He pulled out after a few pumps and he flipped me over and pulled me to the edge of the bed. He placed my feet on his shoulders and slammed back into me. I let out a scream and grabbed his arms.

"Oh, master! Yes, master yes!" I cried.

He pulled out and laid on the bed, "Get on top of me now," he demanded.

I crawled to him and straddled him. I began to go up and down and back and forth. I grabbed the headboard and started to pick up the pace as he closed his eyes and grabbed my ass. He began to move with me, and moans kept escaping both of us. He held my ass and rolled us over as he started to choke me, and I started to cum.

"M---master, I--I'm ab--about to c—cum," I said through the choke hold.

"Cum for me, pisoi. I'm about to cum as well," he said as he pumped one last time, releasing his cum inside me.

As we both came, I felt a short sharp pain in my neck then another wave of high hitting me. He began to cum again with me and we both let out a howl and I arched my back as another one hit me. I screamed unable to help but give everything to this man. He was my safe place, my hide away from the world. He pulled out and laid down next to me. We took a deep breath together. My body finally wasn't on fire anymore. I closed my eyes to savor what just happened and when I opened them and looked at Carson, he was already watching me. I gave him a smile and cuddled up next to him, he wrapped his arms around me and kissed the top of my head.

"That was amazing. How do you feel, love?" he asked.

"It was amazing. I feel great. I did not think it could get

better, but oh my God, it does," I said as I wrapped my arms around him.

He let out a chuckle and wrapped me up tighter. "I had no control over myself, that was all Zeus. I hope he didn't hurt you."

"He didn't hurt me, but he did bite my neck. Noah was in control over me as well," I said as I drew hearts on his chest with my finger.

"It didn't hurt that much; it was more pleasure than pain," I added quickly.

"Are you sure? I don't want him to hurt you," he said as he took my face to meet his.

"Yes, it was amazing. I feel so much more connected to you. I feel safe and at home now that we are one," I said as I looked him in the eyes.

"As long as you are okay, then I'm okay." He kissed me on my lips.

We cuddled and eventually drifted to sleep. Before I lost consciousness to sleep, I couldn't help but think that I was so happy that I was mated to him. I knew that things would get rougher, but we would be together for a long time. After all the happy thinking, I got pulled into a dream that was more of a nightmare.

I was in a room that was covered in blood and Carson was on the floor. He had blood all over him and he wasn't breathing. I ran to him to see how much blood he'd lost and saw that he had a big open wound on his stomach, and he had no heartbeat.

I was woken up by a shake. I opened my eyes to see Carson looking down at me.

"Wake up, sleepy head." He kissed my lips and climbed out of the bed.

"What's going on? Can't we stay in bed today?" I asked, not wanting to get up.

"We have a few more packs coming. Why do you want to stay in bed, love?" He pulled a shirt over his head and pulled a pair of sweatpants on.

"I'm a bit sore from last night," I said as I pulled the covers over my head.

"Why don't I run you a bubble bath with some bath salts and I'll even put a bath bomb in?" he asked as he rubbed my back.

"Mm…that sounds so nice, please if you don't mind?" I asked pulling the covers away.

"Yes, I can do that," he chuckled as he walked to the bathroom.

I heard the water running and the smell of chamomile and sage from the bubble bath. I got out of the bed and headed into the bathroom to see the tub filled with water and filled with bubbles to the top. I undressed and climbed into the tub and laid back. I closed my eyes and took in the warm water.

"Do you like it?" he asked.

"Yes, very much. I just want to soak here for a few if you don't mind. Just tell everyone that I will be out soon," I told him with my eyes closed.

"I will, don't you worry about a thing. You soak and relax," he said as he kissed my head.

I sunk lower in the bath and soaked up the smells while feeling the bubbles all around me. I wanted to turn on the jets, but he had put too many bubbles in the tub. I decided that I'd wait until some went down to turn them on. I closed my eyes and let the bubbles get in my hair. I must have gone to sleep because I got sent into the house that I grew up in.

I looked to my right and saw my dad standing by the balcony looking out towards the garden. Waylon came up behind him and grabbed a cigarette from my dad and stood there for a few minutes.

"What do we have in the North?" my dad asked Waylon.

"Nothing out of order, sir," Waylon said.

"Is that so? Well, I will need to tell my daughter that," my dad said as he turned around.

"Why do you need to tell her? She's just a girl." Waylon finished his cigarette.

"She is the next Alpha and she will have a power that no one had ever seen before," Dad said as he walked to the door.

"Claudia, please come here," he called for me.

"Are you sure she will have a mate? What if her mate is a lot older than her?" Waylon asked.

I try not to gag. I saw my dad's face change. "You will not touch her. You are not her mate and I know that because of the way she looks at you, like an uncle," Dad growled at Waylon.

"Yes, Daddy?" my fourteen-year-old self, interrupted. "Hello, Uncle Waylon," I said as I came out from the house.

I opened my eyes to see Lavender, Abby, and the girls from all the packs had surrounded me. I moved the bubbles closer to me, so I was less exposed. It was weird because they have seen me naked, but I felt like I needed to.

"What's going on? Is everything okay?" I asked them, looking around.

"Everything is fine. We thought maybe you needed some girl time and a break from all the guys," Millie said as she looked out the window to the back yard.

"That sounds nice, thank you. I want to tell you about the dreams that I've been having and what happened last night, too," I said as I sat up a bit.

"We're listening," Abby said.

I told them about the castle and our great grandfather and mother and then I told them how my body was on fire. I told them that Carson and I had sex and that he bit me on the opposite side of my neck from where my mark was. I also told them about what happened in my last dream with my dad and Waylon.

When I finished, I looked at the girls and saw them all speechless. I could feel that I was not as sore as I was earlier. I found the plug and I pulled it letting the water drain and all the bubbles, too. I stood up and made my way to the shower to wash off the soap.

"That's a lot to take in. What do you make of this?" Willow asked as they all looked at the shower door, as I rinsed off.

"I'm not really sure, but I think it's to help fight Waylon and whoever he's making fight with him," I said as I turned off the shower and stepped out.

"That would make a lot of sense," said Brooklyn.

I grabbed the towel that Jessie was holding out for me and wrapped it around myself. I had so many questions about what was going on. The only one that I could think of to help get answers, was Lavender. I just needed to get her alone. I'd have to do that after everyone went to bed.

She could summon demons and enter dreams, not like most wolves. There was only a few of us that had abilities, Lavender, Bleu, me and Millie were the only ones that I knew of that had abilities like that. I thought Willow had it, but I couldn't be sure. I also thought Carson had some too, but I wasn't sure about that, either.

I walked into Carson's room and grabbed my bra and one of his shirts. I pulled on my underwear and a pair of his shorts. I slipped the clothes on and slid my shoes on. I brushed my hair and pulled it into a messy bun. I turned to face the girls and they gave me a nod of approval.

"Okay, let's get this going. I'm ready to kick Waylon's ass," I said as I opened the door and walked out.

"Should we tell her?" Willow said to everyone.

"Well, she's about to find out," they all said.

I walked out to see some chick trying to wrap her paws around Carson.

I walked over and looked at her without saying a word.

"Oh, can I help you?" she said as she looked me up and down.

"Yeah, you can get off my mate," I said through a growl.

"Or, what?" she asked with a grin.

"Or I will make you get off and it won't be nice," I said as I tried to control my temper.

She let out a laugh and tried to grab Carson again. Carson untangled himself and said, "I told you before that I have a mate and I will never want you. She is my mate and isn't afraid to kick your ass or kill you." She let go and gave out a huff.

"Who are you anyway?" I asked, looking at her trying not to kill her.

"I belong to Ashton." She rolled her eyes at me.

"I didn't ask that, I asked for your name," I said rolling my eyes back.

"My name is Cecelia." She smiled as she said her name.

"Never heard of you before," I said.

"I'm Ashton's mate," she said looking at him.

Before I could say anything to that, I saw Millie grab the slut by her throat. She dragged the bitch outside, and we all followed. Millie threw her across the yard and Cecelia hit her head on a tree stump. I tried to stop Millie, but she gave me a look that I had myself when it came to Yasmeen. Just because we are werewolves doesn't mean that we don't have whores too.

I took a step back and let her have it. She grabbed the girl by the hair and dragged her all over the yard. Millie let her go and Cecelia got up and went after Millie. Millie shifted into a small gray and white wolf with blue eyes.

Cecelia shifted into a small brown wolf with green eyes. Millie started to circle Cecelia and studied her. Cecelia attacked her by going for her back. Millie moved to her right and rolled quickly to grab Cecelia by the neck. She held Cecelia until she stopped moving. Millie let her go and backed up. Cecelia shook her neck and went after Millie's legs.

Millie kicked Cecelia with her back legs and sent her flying to the other side of the yard. Cecelia got up and started limping, Millie ran full speed and hit her on the side. I decided that it was time to end it. I shifted and made my way between the two of them. I let out a growl and both stopped at once. We all shifted back, and Mikayla and Bleu went over to Cecelia to help heal whatever injuries she might have sustained.

"Put her in the cells. I will talk to her when she heals," I told Mikayla and Bleu.

I walked over to Millie to help calm her down. I grabbed her by the arm and walked her over to a part of the yard where no one was.

"What was that all about?" I asked her a bit confused. I'd never seen her like that.

"She's tried to get with Ashton multiple times, and I told her to get the fuck away from him, but I guess she didn't get it. She's from a small pack near us, that's all I know about her." Millie started to pace back and forth.

"Well, we don't need to cause anymore friction at this moment with the war that is already ahead of us," I said as I watched her start to calm down.

"I know, I'm sorry. I've just I had enough of her." She walked up to me.

"It's okay. Let's get the meeting of the other packs out of the way." I gave her a hug.

We walked back to the others and saw that a pack from

the West had come to hear what we had to said about joining the war. Carson and I took turns explaining everything, I also told everyone about the dreams I'd been having.

"Waylon tried to force himself to become your mate?" Sam asked.

"Yes, it all makes sense, now. He would always be very touchy-feely with me. I would always tell him to stop. He would only stop when my dad or Paul would come in the room," I informed him.

"That makes me want to rip him to pieces," Paul growled.

"Soon enough, but for now we need to get as many wolves as possible. No matter the size, we need as many as we can get for Waylon to see that he won't win," I said to him.

"You have my vote, Alpha Claudia," Alpha Cole said to me.

"Thank you, Alpha Cole. How about you Alpha Elliot?" I said as I turned to my right.

"I will always be on your side like I was on your dad's side," Alpha Elliot said, giving me a nod.

"Who do we still need?" Carson asked me.

"We need Alpha Felix and that will be it," I told him while looking at everyone.

"That won't be a problem. I heard the news from other wolves and wanted to check it out for myself," Alpha Felix said as he walked up.

"I never liked Waylon and I hate him even more knowing what he did to you when you were younger," he said, spitting at the ground.

I could feel Carson's temper through our mate bond. I looked over to see him looking at me and his look softened when he saw me looking at him. I walked over to my brother and wrapped my arms around him. With us being so close, I could feel him beginning to worry, too. He wrapped his arms around me like he did when I was little and scared. He put his face in my hair like he used to and took a deep breath.

"Everything will be okay. It's not your fault, big brother. If you and Dad knew, he wouldn't even be here today. Please don't blame yourself. I know you worry about me too much," I whispered to Paul as we hugged each other.

"Thank you, my Lilly Pad. I will always worry about you. You are my baby sister after all. I love you, Claudia Lillie Stonewell," he said, his face still in my hair.

"I love you too, Paul Joel Stonewell," I told him, pulling away a bit.

We smiled at each other and I felt a sense of calm wash over me.

As Paul and I stood there wrapped in a hug like old times, I got pulled into a flashback. It was a time when I couldn't sleep, and Mom and Dad were out of town. There was a thunderstorm, and I was about seven at the time. I ran into Paul's room and jumped in bed with him and cuddled up in the covers with him.

"It's going to be okay Lillie; we are safe here. You can always come to me anytime you're afraid," he said to me as we watched the storm until I fell asleep.

I remembered that day like it was yesterday. He always had my back and still did when I needed him. The love we had for each other was unbelievable. I suddenly got sent to a time where I was seventeen and crying over my date to prom because he told me he didn't want to go with me.

"You don't need him. Come on, I have someone you can go with," Paul said as he helped me up. We walked to a tall very handsome guy with tattoos up his arms and jet-black hair and beautiful blue eyes.

"Claudia, this is my good friend Sam. I asked him to take you to your prom," Paul told me.

"Hi, it's nice to meet you," I said.

"Hello, nice to meet you as well." He gave me a smile and I almost melted right there.

Sam was my first real kiss. We secretly saw each other until Paul found out and said that we should stop. We would only go for walks and talk, nothing bad and maybe steal a kiss here or there. Carson was the only guy I'd truly been with and my first for everything except the kiss.

I got pulled into another flashback. Paul and I were playing in a maze with two other kids but for some reason I didn't know who they were. Every time they spoke it was muffled.

"You're going to be okay Lillie," Paul told me.

"Are you sure? Who are they?" I asked him.

"Yes, I'm sure, they are friends of Mom and Dad," he told me.

I looked at the two kids and told them my name. I couldn't hear their names. I looked to Paul and he gave me a small smile. We walked outside to see a big maze and one of the kids ran into it. Paul ran in after him and the other kid ran after him leaving me outside the maze. I took off running into the maze. I caught up to the kid that left me behind. The kid took my hand and led me around the maze.

I then got sent to a flashback of Mom and Dad taking me

to Lavender's mom. Paul and Lavender helped me calm down and relax. I was told to sit in a chair and not move.

"Sweetie, this won't hurt. I need you to close your eyes and take a deep breath," Lavender's mom said to me.

"Okay..." I said looking at my mom and dad.

"She won't remember anything of the meeting of the boys, right?" my mom asked.

"No, she will not remember anything," Lavender's mom said.

"Is this really what you want to do to our daughter, Amelia?" my dad asked my mom.

"Yes, I don't want her to know about the other royal family that is here, Frankie," my mom told my dad.

"What are they talking about brother?" I ask looking at Paul.

"I'm not sure, Lillie," he responded.

"Are we still doing this?" Lavender's mom asked.

"Yes, do you have a problem with this Tulip?" my mom asked her.

"No, I just want to make sure it's a go," Tulip said.

"Just make it quick. I don't want anything left behind," my mom told her.

"Yes, of course." Tulip nodded her head and turned to me.

I closed my eyes. I felt a pull and then everything was hazy. I didn't know what was going on. The pull got a lot stronger and my stomach started to get upset. I wanted to throw up, but I kept everything in. I then felt a haze wash over me and everything became muffled and I couldn't tell who was who. I couldn't tell what was what. The only thing I could hear clearly was my breathing and heart.

"Do you know that her mate is one of these boys?" Tulip asked my mom and dad.

"What?" my parents asked.

"Yes, she is mated to the oldest. She will still be mated to him. I can't take that part away from her. All I can do is have her not remember him and she will have to find him later when she is older," Tulip responded.

"Fine, that is fine. Who is the boy?" my mom asked.

"I think his name is Carson, Mom," Paul said to her.

"Hm…He is no doubt her mate?" my dad asked Tulip.

"Yes, no doubt."

"Okay, do what you have to for her to forget her meeting him," he told her. She gave him a nod and continued what she was doing.

I couldn't hear all of what they were saying but I knew they were talking about me. I wished I knew what they were talking about. I wished my mom didn't erase my memory of Carson. I don't blame her for trying to protect me from others, but I just wished it wasn't from him.

I got sent to another flashback. I was about sixteen when I heard there were a few new kids in town. It was right after my parents were killed. It was a living nightmare for Paul and me. I was in the middle of sneaking out of the house when I got a phone call from Paul giving me the news. The things I felt that day were something I didn't want to ever feel again.

I dropped to my knees and screamed. I felt myself about

to shift so I ran out the house with Emmet, Maxi and Marco on my heels. I ran until I couldn't run any more. I came to the clearing and cried and howled. Emmet and Maxi wrapped their arms around me and held me until I stopped. Maxi took off his jacket and gave it to me so I could cover up while Emmet wrapped me in his arms and carried me back to the house.

"We have her, Beta," Maxi informed Paul.

"Thank you. Put her in her room and I'll be there shortly," Paul replied.

Emmet carried me to my room and set me down on my bed. Maxi grabbed the covers and pulled them up to my chin. I managed to give them a smile before they left me in my dark room. A few minutes later, Paul knocked on my door and opened it. He walked in with bloodshot eyes. He looked like hell as he came to sit on the bed with me.

"How are you holding up Lillie?" he asked.

"Like hell. You?" I asked him.

"Same. How long do you need before you take over Dad's spot as Alpha?" he asked me.

"I'll be ready as long as you are by my side as Beta," I replied.

"Of course, I will be your Beta. I won't leave you, sis. I love you Lilly Pad." He smiled at me.

"Give me until tomorrow. I love you too, Pauly," I smiled back at him.

He stood up to leave, but I grabbed his arm. "Don't leave me please, Pauly?" I pleaded to him with tears falling from my eyes.

"Okay, Lilly Pad. I won't," he said as he laid down. I fell asleep. That night was the start of my nightmares. If it wasn't Paul, it was Emmet or Maxi who ran in to see if everything was okay as I screamed and thrashed around in my sleep. It finally stopped last year, and everyone was happy, but right before Carson called to set up the meeting, they started up again.

This time, when they came back, it wasn't as bad as before. Paul only came into the room once. Lavender was able to make me something to drink to help with the nightmares. She did that up until the day Carson and I met a few days ago, when they disappeared again.

I pulled away from Paul once the flashbacks stopped to see a few tears forming in his eyes. He must have seen them as well. I reached up and wiped them away. I hated seeing him cry. It made me want to do anything to stop the tears from falling.

I LOOKED over to see Claudia in the arms of Paul. I felt help-less and weak. I looked over to Harper and mind-linked with him.

"Frate (brother)?" I called to him.

"Da (yes)?" he responded.

"Casa bunicii iti aduci aminte (grandmother's house, do you remember)?" I asked him.

"Da, de ce (yes, why)?" He looked at me.

"Waylon a venit la casa si a vorbit cu mama si tata (Waylon came to the house and talked to Mom and Dad). El a vrut sa stie daca avem o sora si Mama a spus nu (He wanted to know if we had a sister and Mom said no)," I told him.

"Da, Mama a fost suparata (yes, Mom was mad)," he said, and I suddenly got pulled into a flashback of that day.

I saw Waylon talking to my mom and dad. I could see my mom getting ready to rip Waylon's head off and to the right of them I saw Harper and I playing with each other. I could tell that Dad wanted to kill Waylon as well but the only thing that stopped them was us.

"Do you have a daughter?" Waylon asked.

"No, we have two sons. Why do you ask?" my mom replied.

"I found a little wolf that is a girl in between both of your sons age. She is going to be a very powerful wolf when she gets older," he said looking at Harper and me.

"No, but we would like to meet this little wolf," my dad said.

"Let me call her parents," Waylon said as he flipped up his phone. He walked way for a few minutes while talking to someone on the phone.

"They'll be here shortly," Waylon said as he walked back to my parents.

My mom and dad gave him a nod and my mom told us that we will have company over soon. A short time later, a beautiful flaming red headed girl in pigtails showed up. She had the most beautiful purple eyes on earth. She had a cat shirt and jeans with sneakers on. Beside her was a boy with brownish red hair. He was a bit older than me with a tank top, jeans, and sneakers on.

They were holding hands and he was telling her it was okay. I got this weird feeling in my stomach that I had never felt before. My mom and dad went up to her and the four of them went into the other room leaving Harper, the girl, her brother and myself.

"Hello, my name is Carson, and this is my brother, Harper. What is your name?" I asked them.

"Hello, my name is Paul, and this is Claudia. She's a bit shy," the boy said.

"Nice to meet you guys," Harper said, and I smiled.

"Do you want to play in the gardens? We have a big maze," I told them.

"Sure, I'd love that," said the girl named Claudia.

"Me too!" Paul agreed.

We got up and headed out to the gardens. Claudia and Paul saw the maze and their jaws dropped as they both got excited. Harper took off and ran into the maze. Paul took off after him, then I went. I heard a scared voice behind me. I turned around to see Claudia running up and grabbing my shirt. I took her hand and lead her through the maze. I felt a connection between us. Little did I know, her parents would take her to a witch to get her memory wiped and she wouldn't recall the meeting.

I knew she was my mate when I met her that day when I was twelve and she was ten. I needed to talk to her friend, Lavender, and see if she could unlock those memories for her or if they were lost forever. I would love for her to know that we had met before.

"Frate, esti bine (brother, are you alright)?" Harper asked me.

"Da, doar amintesc vremurile bune (yes, just remembering the good times)," I replied.

"Doar verifcandu-va (just checking on you)," he replied back.

"Multumesc, trebuie sa sunam la o intalnire (thank you,

we need to call a meeting)," I told him as I walked over to Claudia.

"Da, cand doriti sa aveti intalnirea (yes, when do you want to have the meeting)?" he said walking to his mate.

"Maine, am nevoie de somn (tomorrow, I need some sleep)." I ran my hands through my hair.

"Da." He nodded his head.

I wrapped my arms around Claudia and took in her amazing smell.

She turned around and gave me a big smile and I melted right there in her arms. She was the only one I'd ever wanted. When I turned eighteen, I set out to find her. I took my uncle's pack when found out that her pack was close to his. I waited for a few years until I decided to ask for a meeting. Yeah, I fucked around with other girls to get my mind off her, but it didn't work. When I saw her at that restaurant all those feelings came back, and I had to stop myself from telling her how much I loved her.

I wanted to claim her so bad that day, but I knew that it was a bad idea, but still, I couldn't help it. When we kissed, I felt things that I had never felt before. My body felt a charge and it began to hum. I had to stop myself and I could tell she felt it too because she pulled away with the same look that I had on my face.

I was pulled back by Claudia giving me a tug on the arm, "Hey are you okay?" she asked.

"Yeah, just thinking about the first time we kissed. I had to stop myself from taking it too far. I also felt my body hum slightly," I told her.

"I felt it too, but I thought it was just me," she told me.

I wrapped my arms around her tighter, she nuzzled her head in my chest, "Are you sure you want to fight him?" she asked me.

"Yes, if it comes to it. I need to talk to Lavender about something. Can you have her come to my office later today?" I asked.

"Yes, I can do that. Is everything okay?" She looked up at me.

"Yes, love. Just need to ask her a few questions. That's all." I gave her a kiss on the lips savoring her sweet taste.

"Oh, okay. I can ask her to meet you in your office before dinner," she said as she kissed me back.

"That sounds great, my love," I smiled at her.

We looked over to see everyone talking and getting to know each other. I saw a smile forming on Claudia's face. I smiled as well. Felix and Sam are talking. Reese and Ashton are also talking, and Wen, Elliot, and Cole are chatting like they've known each other for years. I grabbed Claudia's hand and brought her to the deck.

"Call every Alpha inside so we can do this meeting, love," I whispered her in her ear.

"Okay, let's do this," she nodded.

"All Alphas, you are needed inside the house for a very important meeting," she called out, grabbing the rest of the Alphas' attention.

We all walked inside and into my meeting room so that we could get the ball rolling.

19

C A R S O N

WE SAT down around the table and it reminded me of King Arthur's round table. We sat accordingly, Claudia at the head of the table and me to the right of her.

We gave our attention to Claudia and I could tell she was nervous. I grabbed her hand and gave it squeeze as Sam grabbed her other hand and did the same. She took a deep breath and nodded her head. She still looked nervous, but I could tell she felt better knowing that we all had her back, no matter what.

"I've never done this so please be patient with me. I've seen my dad do them, but he never let me handle a meeting before," she started as she looked around the room.

"We are here to talk about what actions to take in order to deal with the Waylon situation and the war. Are you ready to fight? Raise your hand if you are."

Half of the group raised their hands while only Cole and

Reese chose not to raise their hands. We put our hands down and looked at Claudia.

"What would you like to do with Waylon, Reese and Cole?" she asked them.

"I think we should hear him out," Reese told us.

"I think we should form an army and let him think about what he's up against," Cole said.

Everyone looked at Claudia. She nodded and then she leaned back in her chair. "I like everyone's feedback. We can hold off on fighting for now, but we will continue to build an army. If he doesn't get the message, then we will have to kill him," she told everyone.

Everyone nodded their understanding.

"Are there any other matters that anyone wants to talk about?" she asked us.

"The attacks on the wolves in the Midwest are getting worse. We're going to need help with putting a stop to it," Ashton said.

"Who is making the attacks?" Wen asked.

"I don't know. We can't figure it out. None of my wolves have been killed, but they have been hurt," Ashton confided.

"You don't think it could be Waylon?" Sam asked.

"No, I don't think so. After the attacks, there's always this green and black substance everywhere when it happens. I also smell sulfur," Ashton informed us.

"That sounds like a demon or Fae attack," Cole said.

"That's what I was thinking. I will grab a few of my pack and send them to check it out," Claudia said.

"Thank you. It means the world to me," Ashton told her.

"Any other matters that need to be talked about?" she asked.

We looked around at each other and saw that Reese had his hand raised. She gave him a nod as to tell him to go on.

"I'm having something similar happen in my territory, but I haven't seen this creature before. It leaves a red, blue and yellow slime behind. The noise that comes from this thing is something I have never heard before. It's like a howl but then it had a sound of a Fae, I think," he told us.

"Do you have any evidence of this?" Felix asked him.

"Yes, I do," Reese said as he pulled out a plastic bag filled with slime that was different colors.

"I will take this and run some test on it," Elliot told him.

"Thank you, that will be really helpful," Reese said.

"Let us know what you find. We will want to know if there is something out there that we don't know about so we can be prepared for it," I told them.

"I agree with Carson. We should all be aware of what's out there and what's going on," Claudia told everyone.

Everyone nodded their heads. Claudia started to talk about how we would lay out everyone and where to meet Waylon. We decided on having mine and Claudia's pack leave first and then send in Ashton's and Sam's packs. Wen and Reese would fill the cracks that were left and have Felix, Cole, and Elliot come up the back and on both sides.

First, we were going to give Waylon a chance to explain all of this and hear him out. If he decided to not comply then we would attack by having Claudia and me go in first. The others would only join if we needed help. No one was to attack until told otherwise.

We didn't want to start anything until he gave us a reason to. We sent a letter as to where to meet. We decided on the meadow clearing in the woods. It was big enough for a fight if needed and big enough to fit everyone. It was also close to the house so we could put the wounded there if we needed to.

"Where is that girl that Millie almost killed and is, she healed up yet?" Claudia asked.

"She's still in the cells and she should be healed. Bleu and Mikayla were working on her," said Ashton.

"Carson can you call someone to bring her in here?" Claudia turned to me and asked.

"Of course, love, is there anything else you need?" I asked her.

"Oh, some chocolate covered gummy bears would be nice," she told me, as she gave me a smile.

I let out a laugh and nodded my head. "I'll ask Nikko to bring both and some snacks for us guys," I told her.

I got up and walked to the door, I opened it up and went to find Nikko. It didn't take long to find the guys in the game room playing videogames on the Xbox One. They looked at me as I walked in.

"Meeting over?" Harper asked.

"No, I need to borrow Nikko," I told them.

"What is it that you need me to do?" Nikko asked.

"I need you to bring the girl that is in the cells to the meeting room and I also need you to bring chocolate covered gummy bears for Claudia and some snacks for the guys," I told him, rolling my eyes.

"Wait, my sister wants the gummy bears?" Paul asked from the couch.

"Yes, why?" I ask, shrugging my shoulders.

"She doesn't eat them. She's not a big fan of them," he told me.

"That's odd. It's what she asked for," I told him.

He shrugged and went back to playing the game. I turned to see that Nikko was leaving so I followed him just in case he needed help with anything. We grabbed the girl and headed to the kitchen and grabbed the snacks for everyone.

We got to the meeting room and Nikko went to leave when Claudia said, "Don't go. You will be bringing her out after we are done with her."

"Yes, Alpha," he responded.

I placed the snacks on the table and the plate filled with the gummy bears in front of Claudia. She grabbed a few and shoved them in her mouth. She chewed them like they were the best thing ever as she grabbed a few more.

"What is your name and what pack do you belong to?" Felix asked the girl.

"My name is Cecelia, I belong to the Greenwells pack," she told everyone.

"What business do you have with Claudia and Carson?" Cole asked next.

"Waylon had asked me to get information on what they are doing," she said.

"Why does he want information and what is going to use it for?" Elliot said next.

"He wants Claudia. He wants to mark her and make her his mate," she responded.

"How will he take Claudia away?" Sam asked before I could.

"Kill her mate and anyone who stands in the way," she said as she looked around.

"What else does Waylon have you doing here?" Wen asked.

"He wants information on the packs that are siding with her and their Alphas," she responded looking down.

"Why does he want to know what Alphas are on her side?" Ashton asked.

"To know if it's worth a fight or if he should play friendly," she told us.

"So, he does want to fight?" Reese asked.

"Only if he thinks it's best," she said.

"How will he get Claudia if he doesn't fight?" I asked, unable to hold my fury back.

"He will take her when no one is looking. He would rather get to her without fighting," she said.

"That will never happen, I'm always with someone wherever I go. Good luck with that," Claudia said as she picked up the last bit of gummy bears.

The girl Cecelia looked at her and said, "He will find a way, he always gets what he wants."

"Nikko put her back in the cells. We will go over what she

said and make a decision on what to do with her," Claudia said, dismissing the girl.

"Yes, Alpha," he said as he grabbed Cecelia and dragged her out of the room.

I looked over to see the gummy bears all gone and Claudia eating the other sweets that I had brought in. I shook my head and made a mental note to ask her if she is feeling alright.

"So, what do you think about what she said?" she asked the room.

"I think we should kill her," Cole said.

"I think we should let her rot in the cells," Reese said.

"I think we should let her be a spy for us," Elliot said.

"I think we need to let her sit in the cells until this is all over with," Felix said.

"I like Felix's idea." Sam, Ashton, Wen, and I agreed.

Claudia sat back and listened to everyone's thoughts on the matter. We sat there without saying a word for about ten minutes. I looked at the table in the room and realized that Claudia had eaten almost all the snacks. I decided to get some snacks before she ate them all. A few of the other guys grabbed some too and we ate, leaving only the sound of food being chewed.

After what felt like years Claudia finally said, "We will go with Felix's idea. I don't like her, but I don't think she should have to die."

We looked at her and nodded our heads to let her know that we all agreed with her. We continued to talk and make suggestions on what to do with Waylon and if we should kill him or let his own ignorance be what killed him. We also made the choice to split everyone up between houses.

Claudia, me, Sam and Ashton would be at her pack house. Reese, Wen, Cole, Felix, and Elliot were to stay here at my pack house.

We finally got up to leave the room so that we could let the packs know the living arrangements. We made our way into the living room to make our announcements. Everyone was standing around the room and waiting to hear how the meeting went.

"We have some things to tell everyone so listen carefully," Claudia said.

"My pack and Ashton's pack will be staying with Claudia and Carson at Claudia's house," Sam said to everyone.

"Yes, and my pack along with Elliot's, Cole's, Wen's, and Reese's pack will stay here in Carson's house," Felix added.

Everyone nodded their heads and made their way to their Alpha. We all separated and made our way to the various houses and rooms. Claudia, Sam, Ashton, and I made our way to Claudia's house, along with our packs.

When we finally got into Claudia's room, I decided to ask her if everything is okay with her. She'd been snacking a lot and eating things she normally didn't like, which was strange to me.

"Hey, is everything okay with you?" I asked.

"Yes, why do you ask?" she said as she walked to the bed.

"You just seem off and your brother said that you don't care for gummy candy. You ate all of it and the rest of the sweet snacks that where on the table at the meeting," I said to her.

"I was just craving them that's all," she said as she crawled into bed.

"Are you sure that it's not something else?" I asked. I had a feeling that something else could be happening here.

She looked at me like I had ten heads. "I don't think so. Why?" she asked me.

"Nothing just making sure that you are okay. I love you," I told her.

"I love you too, Carson. I'm alright. I just wanted some sweets that's all," she said as she kissed me.

I totally lose myself when we kissed. Everything else faded away. I loved her with everything in my body. I pulled her closer and deepened our kiss. She climbed on top of me and her hair fell over our faces. I grabbed her pretty little ass and gave it a squeeze. She let out a moan and kissed me more hungrily. I squeezed it again and moved my kisses to her neck.

I rolled us over so that I had her on her back, and I moved the kisses to her chest and kissed each beautiful titty. I moved one hand to her sweet spot between her legs, and the other to cup her breast. I moved to the left and began to lick and nip at it and with the other hand I began to rub her clit.

She began to moan and said my name as I moved to her right nipple. When I was done with her chest, I moved my kisses down to her sweet spot. I started to kiss both of her inner thighs. She started to moan and move as I got closer to her sweet spot. I drew the letter R with my tongue. She went wild as I began to take my two fingers and move them in and out of her. I played with her clit with my tongue as she grabbed my hair and started to scream, "Master, yes! Oh, God yes!"

She got louder and her body went crazy. I finger fucked her until she came. I stopped eating her out and started to finger the shit out of her.

"Master, yes!" she said.

"You like this?" I asked her as I started to pick up speed.

"Yes, master yes!" she yelled.

I smiled as I made my fingers go in circles and I added a third finger and went faster. Her body arched and her eyes rolled into the back of her head.

I could feel that she wanted to cum, so I slowed down, and I heard her say, "Please master, let me cum please."

"Oh, I don't think so," I told her as I added a fourth finger.

I picked up speed again and I added my last finger and begin to fist fuck the shit out her. She arched her back and rolled her eyes as she shakes.

"Cum for me little one," I commanded her.

She came but I still didn't stop. I fisted her for another ten minutes. I finally stopped and let her get her breath and before I could do anything, she put my penis in her mouth and started to suck on it. I rolled my head back and let out a moan myself. She always knew how to make me go wild.

After a short while she stopped with a big grin on her face. I grabbed her and made her get on her hands and knees with her ass up in the air. I slammed into her letting her know that she would always be mine. I went in and out, fast and hard. Her moans got louder with each slam. I pulled out and flipped her over on her back and slammed into once more.

"MASTER!!!" she screamed.

"Yes, little one?" I asked her as one hand went to her neck and the other grabbed the headboard.

"Do not stop, please," she panted as her eyes rolled back and her body arched.

I let out a small laugh and continued to go in and out with speed. I could feel myself about to reach my climax so I went faster, and I could tell she was getting to her climax again as well. I continued to go in and out and she dug her nails into my back. I knew she was coming undone.

"Cum for me little one," I said again.

"Yes, master. Yes!" she said as she came.

We came together and I gave her a kiss as I pulled out. I grabbed her and pulled her close to me. "I love you, Claudia," I said.

"I love you too, Carson," she said before she drifted asleep.

I laid back on the pillow and tried to get some sleep as well. As I drifted off, I started to dream, and it seemed so real.

I was standing on the shore of the beach with Claudia and we were just sitting there talking and laughing. Then, suddenly, it changed 1, and Claudia is laying on the ground, covered in blood.

I woke up in a full sweat. I looked down to see Claudia

still asleep on my chest. I took in her smell and closed my eyes again.

This time, my dream was better.

We were in the back yard with our kids playing and laughing. We looked so happy, carefree and living life to the fullest. Claudia looked like she was pregnant with a third child. She was smiling as she watched the other two as well as me running around and playing.

I woke up to a kiss. I opened my eyes to see Claudia looking at me.

"Well, hello," I said.

"Hey, sleepy head," she giggled.

"What can I do for you?" I asked her as I sat up.

"I made breakfast and you are the only one who didn't eat yet, so I brought some to you in bed," she said as she grabbed the food tray from the bedside table.

"Why thank you, love. So, what's going on today?" I asked as I cut some pancakes.

"Don't you want to talk to Lavender?" she asked me.

"Yes, I do. Let me get dressed and I'll be in the office. Tell her to come in," I said as I stuffed pancake and bacon in my month.

"Okay, I'll let her know. Eat then get dressed, love," she said as she smiled at me.

"I will." I smiled back at her.

Her smile never left her beautiful face as she walked out the room, leaving me to finish eating and get dressed. I finished my food and headed to the closet. I grabbed a pair of blue jeans and a random t-shirt and slipped on a pair of shoes. I walked out of the closet and into the bathroom. I brushed my teeth and ran a comb through my hair and placed it flat.

I walked out of the room and headed to Claudia's office. It is on the other side of the house. I made my way past Mikayla's room where Harper was still sleeping.

I got to the office and turned on the computer to let it warm up. I decided to look for a book to help unblock memories. It could help both Lavender and me with getting Claudia's memories back that were being blocked. I couldn't find anything, though. Nothing that could help us anyway. I made a mental note to make my way upstairs to the library to see if there might be a book on it.

I heard a knock on the door. "Come in," I said.

Lavender opened the door and walked in and gave me a smile. "Claudia said you wanted to talk to me about something," she said.

"Ah yes, about that. I wanted to ask you about if you know anything about unblocking memories?" I asked, walking to the desk.

"Oh, I can but why are you asking me this and not Claudia?" she asked a little confused.

"I don't think she knows that she had a block on her mind," I told her.

"I can tell you that she doesn't. My mother was the one who put the block on her mind. When Claudia said that you where her mate, I knew it was going to be a matter of time before I should take the block off. I always struggled with telling her about it sooner, but I figured that our parents had a good reason for it," she told me as she sat down.

"Really?" I couldn't think of anything else to say.

"Yes, really. She'll have to be asleep for me to do it without her knowing," she said to me.

"Okay, is there anything that you need from me?" I asked her.

"No, just ask her to go to sleep early and by tomorrow she should get the memories that are blocked, back. She will be a little off but should be back to her old self in the next few days," she told me.

"Okay, I can do that," I told Lavender knowing that there was only one thing that would make Claudia go to sleep early. Sex.

She stood up and walked to the door. "I will be getting ready for tonight."

I nodded my head and brought my attention to the computer when Claudia mind linked me. "Carson, I need you to come here now! Please!" she said.

I stood up and asked, "Where are you pisoi?"

"The bathroom in our room," she told me.

I rushed out of the office and ran down the hall and into the bedroom, I could see the bathroom door open. I walked in to find Claudia on the floor by the toilet.

"What's going on pisoi?" I asked, kneeling down beside her.

"Look," she said as she pointed to the sink.

I stood up and looked on the sink to find a pregnancy test sitting on it. I looked closer to see that it read positive. I went and sat on the floor by Claudia and said, "We're having a pup?"

"You're not mad?" she asked as she looked at me.

"No, I always wanted a few children and having one with the woman I love is even more special. I'm so excited about this." I wrapped my arms around her and kissed her lips.

She kissed me back and snuggled up against me. I couldn't have been happier. I knew that this only meant that I would have to be extra careful with this war with Waylon, but I knew I would do everything in my power to keep her and our unborn child safe. He would not take my family away from me. Not now, not ever.

To Be Continued…

COMING SOON

Alpha's Moon (Book two)

Stars to the Wolf (Book three)

Many more soon

Made in the USA
Columbia, SC
12 April 2023

14836176R00102